To Mara with love from Robbie

Farewell Innocence

By Roberta Grieve

Roberta Grieve

WL

Books We Love
A quality publisher of genre fiction.
Airdrie Alberta

Digital ISBN 978-1-77299-225-0
Print ISBN 978-1-77299-226-7

Chapter One

Wide-eyed, Ruby Hinton gazed around her at the sumptuous furnishings, taking in the moulded panelling, the crystal chandeliers and the richly-coloured brocade curtains. She could just about remember the last time she had been in this room.

At four years old she had been taken away from her foster mother and brought here to the Foundling Hospital to spend the next twelve years of her life. She could still recall the feeling of bewilderment at being forced to say goodbye to the only mother she had ever known. She remembered, too, the sharp slap that Matron had given her when she started to cry.

She had eventually managed to settle down to her new life and now the motherly woman who had cared for her as a baby was a distant memory. It was only when walking in the grounds of the Foundling Hospital that occasionally a brief scent of blossom from the neighbouring fields would remind her of that country cottage and the happy times she had spent there.

Now it seemed she was to be wrenched away again from a settled and, she had to admit, not too unhappy existence. Who knew what lay in store for her now?

'Stand up straight, Hinton. Pay attention.' The harsh voice brought her wandering thoughts back to the big man sitting behind the desk.

Hands clasped in front of him, the Governor of the Foundling Hospital leaned forward, fixing her with a stern gaze. 'You know why you're here,' he said.

'Yes, sir. I'm to leave the Hospital.' Her voice trembled. Most of the girls her age had left two years ago to go into service. But Ruby had been ill with a debilitating fever which had left her very weak and unable to do physical work. As she had slowly recovered she had been given work in the hospital kitchens. But now, at the age of sixteen, the Matron and Governor had decided it was time she was sent out into the wide world to earn her own living.

'A position has been found for you. The Prestons are a God-fearing family and, if you have learned your lessons here well, I am sure you will be of good service to them. You will start off as a kitchen maid but who knows, with hard work and diligence you may rise to a higher position in time.' The Governor stood up and smiled. 'Take this, my dear, and, if you follow its teachings diligently, I am sure you will benefit from them.' He handed her a small book, leather-covered, the words 'Holy Bible' stamped in gold on its cover.

'Thank you, sir,' Ruby whispered, bobbing a curtsey.

The Governor beckoned to Matron who had been standing quietly behind Ruby. 'Someone is coming for her. Take her upstairs to fetch her things and then go down to the main gate and wait with her, please.'

'Yes, sir.' Matron gave Ruby a little push. 'Go along then. Don't linger.'

Ruby's heart began to beat a little faster. This was it then. She really was leaving the safety of the Hospital, the only home she had known apart from those early years with her beloved foster mother. Of her own real mother she had no memory at all, left at the Foundling Hospital when only a few days old, and lucky to be taken in, as she had constantly been reminded throughout her growing up years.

She had been fed and clothed, taught to read and write a little, to sew and do household tasks in preparation for a life in service. But of warmth and affection there had been little. Ruby could not say she was unhappy but she often thought back longingly to the small cluttered cottage where her foster mother had done her best to care for the four children in her care. She had been one of the lucky ones; others in her dormitory had not fared so well.

Friendships had not been encouraged but she had become fond of Mary, who had slept in the next bed to hers. She was a quiet, shy child who seemed to be frightened of everything. The night before she left she had told Ruby how nervous she was of going to work in the shoe factory with its noisy machinery. Since then, Ruby had had no one to talk to and she had felt very lonely.

Although she too had dreaded being sent out into the world of the unknown, she hoped that it would be for the best. Since recovering from her illness she had been forced to work hard, spending most of her waking hours in the huge kitchens at the rear of the Foundling Hospital, peeling mountains of potatoes and scouring the vast cauldrons with their baked on stew. Surely being a maid in a family home could not be worse than that she told herself as, back in the dormitory, she removed the brown wool dress with its red edging which had been her uniform for all those years.

As she folded it neatly, Matron came in and said, 'Hurry up, girl. I haven't got all day.'

Ruby bit her lip, reluctant to don the grey serge frock and woollen shawl which were laid out on the bed, as the reality of her imminent departure came home to her. She fastened the dress, threw the shawl round her shoulders and picked up the small bag containing a couple of aprons, a mob cap, and a selection of underwear including the unfamiliar corset which she had been told she must wear from now on - the servant's uniform provided by the Hospital for girls going into service.

When she was ready, Matron hustled her downstairs and out of the building to the front gate, tapping her foot impatiently as they waited for the Prestons' housekeeper who was to accompany Ruby to Exton House.

At last a hansom cab drew up at the gates and the woman inside beckoned to Ruby. 'Come along, girl,' she called.

Matron gave Ruby a little push, saying, 'don't forget what you've learned here – duty, obedience.'

'Yes, ma'am,' Ruby replied as she had been taught. She picked up the bag and climbed into the cab. Inwardly, she trembled but she gritted her teeth and determined to look to the future as an adventure. She smiled at the woman who sat opposite, trying to make the best of things. But all she got in return was a hard stare.

As the cab started off, throwing her back in the seat, she had no time to savour the new experience of being carried at speed along the wide road towards the city.

A sharp poke in the ribs made her sit up straight and force her eyes away from the passing scene, fascinating as it was to someone who hadn't been outside the Foundling Hospital for so many years. As they drew nearer to the city centre, the noise and bustle frightened her a little but underneath she felt a little quiver of excitement. Despite her nervousness, she told herself that it was good to be out in the world, free from the restrictions and harsh regime of life in the Foundling Hospital.

'I'm Hetty Catchpole, the housekeeper – but you will call me Mrs Catchpole,' the woman said, interrupting her thoughts. 'I am ultimately responsible for the indoor servants but you will be under Mrs Andrews, the cook. She will explain your duties.'

'Yes, ma'am,' Ruby said.

'Yes, Mrs Catchpole,' the housekeeper corrected her. 'You address Lady Anne as Ma'am, the daughters of the house are Miss, the Master is Sir. Then there's the son – he's come of age now so you call him Mister Oliver.' She paused and pursed her lips. 'The family is away in Scotland at present – due back in a couple of weeks. You will be in the kitchens down in the basement. And you'll use the back stairs to get to your room at night so you're unlikely to come across any of them even when they are in residence.'

'Yes, Mrs Catchpole,' Ruby said, trying to take it all in as the housekeeper went on to tell her about the other servants and what would be expected of her.

'One last thing - if by chance you do come across any of the family you must stand aside, and never ever speak unless you are spoken to.'

'Yes, Mrs Catchpole,' Ruby repeated. She was terrified of forgetting something, convinced that Mrs Catchpole was going to prove a hard taskmaster. It seemed there were as many, if not more, rules and regulations to be observed at Exton House as there had been at the Hospital.

The cab turned into Warwick Square, and Ruby gazed in awe at the tall imposing houses, each with wide steps up to their front doors and tradesman's entrances down in the basement area.

They stopped and Hetty Catchpole once more poked Ruby in the ribs. 'Stop day-dreaming girl. There's work to do,' she snapped.

Ruby grabbed her bag and climbed down from the cab to get her first look at Exton House, her new home. It stood on the corner of the square, larger than the other houses with wooden gates to the side leading to a mews with stables and a coach house.

As she got out of the cab, Mrs Catchpole put her hand up to her chest and turned quite pale. 'What's he doing here again?' she muttered.

Ruby looked round to see someone beside the open gate talking to the coachman. She could tell from his uniform that the taller man was a policeman. She had seen members of the Metropolitan Police calling at the Hospital from time to time when there had been disputes over the admittance of a new child to the home. The other man was obviously the Prestons' coachman.

Ruby felt a little nervous, knowing that where there was a policeman there was usually trouble. Perhaps that was why Mrs Catchpole looked upset, she thought.

The housekeeper let go of her arm. 'Wait here,' she said, striding over to the men. 'Williams, what's going on?' she demanded.

'There's been another burglary. Constable Locker was asking if I'd seen anything suspicious lately,' the coachman replied.

'And have you?' Mrs Catchpole asked.

'No, but I wondered if you might have done.'

'Me? How could I?'

'When you went out last night. I saw you coming back. Quite late it was.'

'I'd been to visit my sister – she's very ill – not that it's any of your business.' She turned to the policemen. 'I saw nothing at all, constable.'

'Thank you anyway, ma'am. But please be on the alert. This is a very dangerous gang and they seem to be targeting houses where the owners are away.'

'Dangerous? What do you mean?'

'They have been known to attack anyone who tries to interfere with them. I have advised Mr Williams and the other servants to report any suspicions to us rather than try to take the law into their own hands.'

'Of course,' Mrs Catchpole said.

Ruby had been listening horrified to this exchange. Burglars, she thought, wishing she was back in the safety of the Foundling Hospital. But the policeman turned to her and smiled.

'Don't worry, miss. I'll be walking my beat round this square tonight. If I see anything suspicious I only have to blow my whistle and plenty of other constables will rush to my aid.'

She felt a little comforted by his words and managed a tremulous smile but before she could reply, Mrs Catchpole gave her a little push and she stumbled down the area steps into the basement kitchen.

'Well, Mrs Andrews, here she is, Ruby Hinton, the new maid,' the housekeeper said. 'I'll leave you to show her the ropes. I've got work to do.' As she was about to leave the room, she turned and said, 'That policeman was outside again, talking to Williams. He's always hanging around here. I'll get Mr Phelps to have a word with him. It looks bad and I'm sure Sir Charles wouldn't be pleased to hear of it.'

'You're worrying about nothing, Mrs C. He's sweet on young Fanny, that's why he stops by so often,' Mrs Andrews said.

'Well, he said he's investigating a burglary near here. Anyway, he won't get far with Fanny. I believe she is spoken for.' And with a sniff of disapproval, the housekeeper swept out of the room, banging the door behind her.

Ruby was still standing by the door, not sure what to do or say and she smiled uncertainly at the large woman who was sitting in a wooden armchair beside the range, fanning herself with a wooden spoon, and occasionally stirring something on the stove.

The room was stiflingly hot, the heat coming from the kitchen range which took up almost all of one wall. Ruby was relieved to see that the kitchen was not unlike that at the Foundling Hospital, although on a smaller scale. With its wooden dresser crammed with plates and dishes and the drying rack over the range it was comfortingly familiar.

'Come along in then – Ruby, isn't it?' The large woman smiled and gestured to her to sit down at the large scrubbed table in the middle of the room.

Ruby nodded and perched on the edge of a chair, her nervousness lessening a little. 'Now, pay attention, Ruby. I don't want to have to keep repeating myself. You will be working with Kitty the other kitchen maid. She'll show you what to do.'

She banged the side of the pot with the spoon and called out, 'Kitty, here girl, you're wanted.'

A small girl with sweat-streaked face and straggly hair escaping from its mob cap, came out of an adjoining room, wiping her hands on her sacking apron. 'Yes, Mrs Andrews. What is it? I haven't finished the potatoes yet. And Annie's still cleaning the silver.'

'Never mind that. This is Ruby the new kitchen maid. She'll help you. But first take her up to your room and show her where to put her things.' She turned to Ruby. 'You'll be sharing with Kitty and Annie. Off you go – and get back down here sharpish. There's lots to do yet.'

Ruby plucked up her courage and spoke out. 'They told me I was going to be a housemaid,' she said.

'I don't know where you got that idea. You've no training have you? Besides, worked in the kitchens at the hospital, didn't you.'

'But…'

'Don't argue, girl. You're here now and you'll do as you're told.' Mrs Catchpole grabbed her arm and gave her a shake. 'Go along now.'

As she followed the other girl out of the kitchen she heard the housekeeper say, 'These girls today. They don't know their place. The cheek of it, questioning me like that.'

Ruby was beginning to wish she was back in the kitchens at the Foundling Hospital but as they hurried along the passage, the other girl said, 'Don't mind her. She's a crabby old thing. And if you're working in the kitchens you won't see much of her anyway. I'm Kitty by the way.'

Ruby smiled, grateful for a friendly face. As they hurried along, past several doors, and up a short flight of steps to a baize door Kitty pointed out the Cook's sitting room, the butler's pantry and other rooms. 'And that leads down to the cellar where they keep the coal,' she said, pointing to a door at the end. 'It's scary down there so we don't go down if we can help it but there are storerooms too so sometimes we have to.

She led the way up the back stairs to the top of the house. 'This is where we sleep,' she said preceding Ruby into a long low room. Three small iron bedsteads were ranged along one wall. In the corner was a scuffed and battered chest of drawers and under the window a wooden chest.

Ruby walked across to the window and stood on tiptoe to look out, her heart lifting at the sight of the treetops stirring in the breeze. 'Is that a park across the road?'

'It's a private garden for the residents of the square – not for the likes of us. The nursemaids from the houses on the other side take the children in there sometimes.'

Ruby sighed. She would miss the gardens at the Foundling Hospital where occasionally she had been sent to pick peas or beans for the kitchens. Still, the sight of the trees lifted her spirits after the hansom cab drive through grey streets of tall buildings.

'Come along,' Kitty said. 'No time for window-gazing. Mrs A will be shouting for us if we don't hurry.' She lifted the lid of the chest. 'Me and Annie share the drawers so you can put your things in there.'

Ruby put her bag down on one of the beds and started to unpack it.

'No, leave it till later. Just put your apron and cap on.' Kitty stood by the door while Ruby got ready. It had not occurred to her that she would be expected to start work straight away with no time for settling in.

They left the attic and Kitty pointed to another door across the passage. 'That's where Prue sleeps, she's a housemaid. She works with Fanny, the coachman's daughter.'

'Why does she have a room to herself and three of us have to share?'

'Housemaids don't share with kitchen maids. You'll learn.'

Ruby bit her lip at the other girl's abrupt tone.

Kitty touched her arm. 'Sorry. But Prue thinks she's a cut above us. Anyway, I don't think she'll be here much longer.'

'Why?'

'You ask too many questions.' Kitty shrugged. 'When you've been here a while you'll realise that housemaids don't last long in this household. Let's hope you get to stay anyway.'

As she hustled Ruby down the back stairs to the basement, she couldn't resist asking one more question. 'Does Mrs Andrews' husband work here too?'

Kitty burst out laughing. 'Bless you, no. She ain't got a husband.'

'But she's called 'Mrs'. Is she a widow then?'

'I can tell you ain't been in service before,' Kitty said. 'Cooks is always called 'Mrs'. Old Hetty - Mrs Catchpole - too.' She stifled a giggle. 'Though who would marry that skinny old thing I don't know.'

Ruby had already formed her opinion of the housekeeper on the drive from the Foundling Hospital but she asked anyway. 'What's she like then?'

'Like I said - a mean old besom, down on you like a ton of bricks if she thinks you're slacking. But don't worry, we don't have a lot to do with her in the kitchen although she's in charge of the indoor staff. Cook's the one we have to please and if we work hard she's all right. Gets a bit short-tempered when there's a big party or something on and there's extra work.'

Kitty opened the baize door and they hurried along the passage to the kitchen.

'Oh, there you are,' Mrs Andrews said. 'Get a move on, then.'

'Yes, Mrs Andrews,' Kitty said meekly. All trace of the lively giggling girl that Ruby had instinctively taken to were gone in an instant. She grabbed Ruby's arm and almost dragged her into the adjoining scullery, where another girl, even smaller and thinner than Kitty, was bent over a bench, rubbing away at a large serving spoon. The smell of silver polish permeated the air.

'Haven't you finished yet, Annie?' Kitty asked. 'Mrs A will be on your back.'

'Nearly done,' the girl whispered with a frightened look at Kitty.

'Don't mind me,' the other girl said. 'I just don't want you to get into trouble.' She pushed Ruby forward. 'This is the new kitchen maid – Ruby. She'll give you a hand while I finish the potatoes.'

Ruby perched on a stool and picked up a polishing cloth. 'They all have to be washed after polishing,' Annie said.

The rest of the morning passed quickly and Ruby was surprised when Kitty announced that it was dinner time. She realised she was very hungry, having only had a small bowl of gruel very early that morning. She wanted to ask what the food was like but didn't dare. Still, she was so hungry she would have eaten anything. It was a pleasant surprise when they were all seated round the big table and Mrs Andrews doled out ladlefuls of fragrantly steaming mutton stew accompanied by big floury dumplings. This was better fare that she was used to and Ruby began to hope that, despite her exhaustion from the unremitting toil of the morning, things would not be too bad.

She was about to dig into her stew when she felt Kitty's hand on her arm. The girl nodded in the direction of the man seated at the head of the table.

'Grace first,' she whispered.

Ruby flushed. She should have known – after all, saying grace and prayers were part of the usual routine where she had come from, but her hunger had made her forget. She bowed her head while grace was said and, glancing round at the others, waited for them to start before picking up her spoon.

The man at the head of the table, who she'd learned from Kitty was Mr Phelps, the butler, cleared his throat. 'I see there is a new face in our midst.' He said, fixing Ruby with a stare.

She coloured and was about to speak when Mrs Andrews said, 'This is Ruby, the new kitchen maid, May's replacement.'

Mrs Catchpole, who was sitting at the other end of the long table, interrupted. 'Do not mention that slut's name here,' she snapped. 'We are well rid of her.'

Mr Phelps glared at her. 'This is not the time or place…' he said, turning to Ruby. 'Welcome to Exton House. If you do your work and follow the rules, you will be happy here I'm sure.'

Ruby nodded. It wouldn't be that much different to her previous life, she thought, although she hoped there wouldn't be quite so many potatoes to peel. But she had a roof over her head and good food as well as the promise of a friend in her fellow kitchen maid.

Chapter Two

Ruby had been at Exton House for two weeks and, as she settled into the routine of the household she was beginning to think it wasn't as bad as she had feared it would be. Kitty had been very kind showing her where things were kept and discreetly putting her right when she could not remember.

So far she had seen little of Hetty Catchpole which suited her very well. She had to admit, she was more than a little frightened of the thin-lipped housekeeper. Luckily, she and Mr Phelps usually only entered the kitchen regions at mealtimes when they presided over the long table and passed on any news of what was going on upstairs.

Mrs Andrews was strict too and very prone to hitting out with her wooden spoon if any of the lower servants were too slow in obeying her commands. But Ruby had soon realised that so long as she did her work to the older woman's satisfaction, she was safe.

'She's all right,' Kitty whispered as they worked alongside each other in the scullery, scrubbing away at the big copper pans. 'Not like that other one,' she added, nodding towards the door.

Mrs Catchpole had just descended to the kitchen, holding Annie by the arm and breathing fire. She had caught the scullery maid creeping up the back stairs to her room in the middle of the day.

Ruby and Kitty listened, stifling their giggles as Mrs Andrews gave as good as she got. 'And what business is it of yours what orders I give my kitchen staff?' she demanded.

'Kitchen staff belong in the kitchen,' Hetty snapped. 'They've no call to go wandering around upstairs in the middle of the day.'

'I sent her up to bed. The girl's got a bad cold and I don't want her sniffling and snuffling over the food.'

'I'd give her something to snivel about if it were up to me,' the housekeeper said, giving Annie a final shake before pushing her across the room. 'Well, she can stay down here now. The family is due back tomorrow and my housemaids don't want to be tripping over her when they're dashing up and down stairs.'

'Have it your way Mrs C,' the cook said.

The door slammed and Ruby eased open the scullery door to see Annie standing with her head bent, tears rolling down her face. 'I'm sorry, Mrs Andrews. I didn't mean to...' the girl sniffed.

'Never mind. Better stay here in the warm anyway. Just keep out of my way that's all.' The cook's voice was rough but there was a hint of kindness in it. 'I've got enough to do with preparing all this food for that lot when they arrive tomorrow.' She waved her wooden spoon in the direction of the steps which led up to the baize door and the Prestons' part of the house.

Ruby bit her lip to hide a grin. Mrs Andrews was quite forthright in her manner but only when neither Mr Phelps nor the housekeeper were within hearing. They were quick to reprimand any of the servants who showed disrespect to their masters. And referring to them as 'that lot' was definitely disrespectful.

She closed the door quietly and the two girls continued with their task. So, the Prestons were due back from their shooting holiday in Scotland, she thought. As Mrs Catchpole had told her, she was unlikely to come across any of them, except for Lady Anne who, she had been told, occasionally descended to the kitchen to consult with Mrs Andrews about menus. But she couldn't help wondering what they were like.

* * *

At dinner time the kitchen filled with the other servants jostling to get round the table. Each had their appointed place and Ruby was careful not to sit in the wrong chair as she had done on her first day here.

Mr Phelps presided at the head of the table, flanked by Silas, the footman and next to him, Jimmy the boot boy. Mrs Catchpole sat at the other end with the housemaids on either side of her. Ruby hadn't had a chance to get to know them yet and Kitty had explained that it wasn't done to get too friendly with the upper maids.

It was a shame, Ruby thought, as one of the girls smiled at her before taking her seat. Fanny Williams looked friendly enough, although she could not say the same for Prue, who always looked miserable and hardly said a word to anyone.

Later, as Ruby and the other two girls cleared away and started on the mammoth task of washing the dishes and scouring the pots and pans, she asked Kitty what was wrong with her.

'I don't know. She used to seem happy enough - she and Fanny were always being told off for chattering. But just lately...'

'Perhaps she's not well,' Ruby suggested. She had seen how Mrs Catchpole felt about the servants being ill from her treatment of Annie. Poor Prue could not expect any sympathy there.

'You could be right. She's been looking a bit peaky lately. I wonder...' Kitty paused with the drying cloth in her hand.

'What?'

Kitty shrugged. 'Oh, nothing.' She finished drying the big meat dish and handed it to Ruby to take through to the kitchen and put on the dresser.

Mrs Andrews was up to her elbows in flour, rubbing in the lard to make pastry. More washing up, Ruby thought, as she was about to return to the scullery.

'Wait a minute, girl. Fetch me that deep pie dish from the store room,' the cook said.

Ruby nodded and scurried down the passage, hesitating in front of the store room door. Yes, it was this one. Thank goodness she was at last learning her way around this warren of basement rooms, she thought. Last week she had opened the wrong door, closing it hurriedly when she realised it was the room where Silas slept. When she had confided her mistake to Kitty, the other maid had laughed.

'You'd be in trouble if you were caught. We're not allowed to enter the men's sleeping quarters and they certainly would be dismissed if they so much as set foot on the attic stairs.'

Ruby sighed. Would she ever get to remember all the many rules and regulations of life below stairs? She lifted the heavy earthenware dish off the shelf and hurried back to the kitchen.

'Good girl,' Mrs Andrews said. 'You're settling in nicely. But you've had it easy these past couple of weeks with the family away. You'll find it very different from tomorrow – parties, dinners – always something.' She added water to the pastry mix and kneaded it with her big meaty hands. 'This pie now – I'm making this specially for Mister Oliver. He does love his pies. The young misses now, they prefer more dainty fare.'

Ruby couldn't agree that she'd had it easy as Cook said. She had been permanently tired since coming to Exton House and couldn't imagine having to work even harder. Oh well,

I'll just have to get used to it, she thought. 'I'll do my best, Mrs Andrews,' she said.

Some of the servants had gone to Scotland with their employers and Ruby wondered if there would be more help in the kitchen when they returned. But when she mentioned it to Kitty as they got ready for bed that night, the other girl gave a scornful exclamation. 'They don't take kitchen staff away with them,' she said. 'It's their personal servants they need when they're staying at the Castle. Lady Anne and the young misses have Gladys, their personal maid, and Sir Charles has his valet, Archie Bass, him that Fanny Williams is sweet on.'

'So where do they sleep then?' Ruby asked. She couldn't imagine there was room for all of them as well as the family despite the impressive size of the five storey house 'Does Gladys share with Prue across the landing?'

'Bless you, no. Miss Gladys Baker is too high and mighty to mix with the likes of us. She has her own little room between her Ladyship and the young misses. That way she's on hand if any of them need anything.'

'And Fanny lives with her family above the coach house, doesn't she?' Ruby sighed enviously. If only she had a family to go home to at the end of a hard day's work.

'And very lucky she is too, to be allowed to,' Kitty said. 'Most households would insist on her living in. But her mother is sometimes poorly and needs help with the little boys. Lady Anne can be very kind – if your face fits.'

Well, Ruby thought, turning her back so that Kitty could help unfasten her stays, Lady Anne might be kind but that Mrs Catchpole isn't. I've seen the way she looks at Fanny - such malice. Perhaps she doesn't like those under her being shown such favour.

She didn't voice the thought though, and taking off her dress, she climbed into bed in her shift, pulling the thin blanket over her shoulder.

In seconds she was asleep and it seemed only a few moments before she was awake again, sitting up and rubbing her eyes as Kitty roughly shook her arm.

'Come on, Rube. Lots to do today. They'll be here at midday and they'll want feeding.'

Ruby leapt out of bed and went across to the wash stand, splashing her face with cold water to try and wake herself up. Kitty helped her to dress and she then took her turn at fastening the other girl's stays.

'If only we didn't have to wear these awful things,' Kitty grumbled.

Annie, who was already out of bed and almost dressed, said, 'I haven't bothered with them.'

'Let's hope Mrs A doesn't notice then,' Kitty remarked.

Ruby wished she was brave enough to flout convention but she dreaded being singled out for attention. But as she tightened Kitty's laces, she thought back longingly to the simple wool dress with its red braid trimming that had been her uniform at the Foundling Hospital.

Downstairs there was scarcely time to eat their porridge before Mrs Andrews was chivvying them to get on and the morning passed in a blur as Ruby scrubbed pans, prepared vegetables and scurried in and out of the larder and store rooms fetching and carrying for the cook.

When Fanny came into the scullery carrying a huge tray full of dirty crockery, Ruby heaved a sigh of relief. The family had finished their luncheon and perhaps the servants would get a chance to sit down and have their meal before the whole long round began again. She was beginning to realise what Mrs Andrews had meant when she said they'd had it easy the past few weeks.

* * *

The next day, Fanny came in wearing a beaming smile. Her day off had obviously done her good for she had been looking very tired with all the running up and down stairs preparing for the Prestons' return.

Kitty enlightened Ruby when the housemaid had left the room saying, 'You can tell Archie's back. She's been quite miserable lately.'

'Are they courting then?'

'Not officially – you know the rule. No followers. But Fanny living at home with her parents has more freedom than the rest of us. And her mum and dad approve of Archie.'

Once again Ruby felt wave of envy, not that she begrudged the other girl a chance of happiness. She just knew it would never happen for her. No, she would be stuck in the basement of Exton House for the rest of her days with no chance of escape, except for being sent on the occasional errand for Cook.

Apart from when the servants had all lined up in the hall to greet the family on their return, she had scarcely seen her employers except for a quick glimpse when she had been summoned to fetch the used tea things from the drawing room.

Before she could ask any more questions, Mrs Andrews called them into the kitchen for their meal, and she hurriedly joined Annie and Kitty at the table.

Mr Phelps had already taken his place and, before grace, he called for silence as he had something important to tell them. He cleared his throat and said, 'It is my sad duty to inform you that Prue has been dismissed without a character.'

'Not another one,' Mrs Andrews exclaimed.

Mr Phelps gave the cook a hard stare and continued, 'She is packing her things and will leave the house immediately. I must warn you that none of you is to have any dealings with her from now on. If you should come across her on your way back to work this afternoon. You must ignore her' He looked at Fanny and she lowered her eyes.

Ruby could see that she had been crying and wondered what the girl could possibly have done to warrant instant dismissal. It must be something really awful, she thought.

As soon as they had finished eating, she took her plate into the scullery and grabbed Kitty by the arm. 'What was all that about? What has she done?'

'Only gone and got herself into trouble, that's what,' Kitty said.

'What sort of trouble?'

Kitty put her finger to her lips as Annie came in bearing a tray laden with dirty dishes. 'I'll tell you later.'

Ruby couldn't imagine what Prue's crime had been unless she had stolen something. And was that why the other maid, May, had been dismissed too? What else could it be? She didn't have a chance to ask as she and the other servants were kept busy all afternoon and when she finally reached the attic after an exhausting day, Kitty had beaten her to it and was already fast asleep.

And when she mentioned it to Annie, the scullery maid shook her head.

'I can't say, Ruby. There's only one kind of trouble girls like us get into. Best not to talk about it.' She lowered her voice to a whisper although there was no chance of anyone hearing her above Kitty's snoring. 'All I can tell you is to keep out of Mister Oliver's way. I'm safe enough but he likes pretty girls – and you're very pretty Ruby.'

* * *

A few days later, Ruby was scrubbing the big deal table in the centre of the kitchen when the bell for the drawing room jangled overhead. She ignored it until Mrs Catchpole rushed in. 'Why doesn't someone answer that bell?' she demanded.

Since the Prestons had returned to London it seemed as if the bells which hung in a row above the big fireplace never stopped ringing. They would just have sat down to supper or tea when one of them would startle them with its harsh jangling and Mr Phelps would despatch one of the servants to find out what was needed.

'It's not the kitchen maid's job to take the tea up,' Mrs Andrews replied.

'Well, there's no one else is there. Fanny's busy. You'll have to send Ruby.'

'It's about time we got a replacement for Prue,' said Mrs Andrews.

The housekeeper's lips tightened, but she did not comment. Instead she turned to Ruby. 'Well, girl. Take the tray up to the drawing room at once.'

Ruby nodded and picked up the heavy tray which had been laid ready for the Prestons' tea. Since Prue left, she had also been given the job of making up the fires, an arduous chore, especially having to carry the heavy coal scuttles up two flights of stairs. But she never minded leaving the kitchen and having the chance to see the rest of the house. The beautiful furnishings and gleaming chandeliers were a welcome change from the dark basement regions where she spent most of her time.

As she struggled up the narrow back stairs with the heavy tray she hoped that Mister Oliver was not at home today. She had encountered him a couple of times on the stairs and, although she did as instructed and kept her eyes lowered as he passed, she was aware of his piercing stare. Once she had caught his eye, purely by accident, and he had smiled at her. Mindful of Annie's warnings, she had quickly looked away, not sure that she liked the glint in his eye.

She was finding the tray difficult to manage and, terrified of breaking the delicate china, she couldn't wait to put it down. As she entered the room she saw to her discomfiture that Oliver was there too. To her surprise he broke off the conversation with his two sisters and stood up to take the tray from her. As he placed it on the table beside Lady Anne, she gave him a disapproving look, but he just smiled.

Flustered, Ruby felt herself blushing. 'Thank you, sir,' she said, looking down at her feet.

'That will be all, Hinton,' Lady Anne said sharply.

Ruby scurried out of the room and ran down the back stairs. She hoped that she would not be asked to do that again. Mister Oliver always seemed nice but no matter how warm his smile, or how handsome he was, she would not do anything to encourage him. To do so would incur Mrs Catchpole's wrath and lead to her dismissal. And despite the unremitting hard work and constant tiredness she was reasonably happy here. She could have ended up in a far worse household, as she realised from the stories she'd heard when the servants gathered for their supper at the end of the day.

Chapter Three

Ruby's content with her lot hadn't lasted long. A replacement housemaid for Prue still hadn't been found and she was having to do more work upstairs as well as helping Mrs Andrews in the kitchen. But despite being constantly tired, she enjoyed working with Fanny and over the past few weeks they had become fast friends.

What she most enjoyed though was the chance to get out of the house. It didn't happen often but sometimes the tradesmen didn't deliver quite what Mrs Andrews wanted and then she would send Ruby to the market. She didn't even mind when it was cold or wet.

And it was on just such a day that Ruby's life changed – and not for the better.

An autumn gale had stripped the leaves from the trees in the square and she hurried along to the market, clutching her shawl around her. She had completed her errand and was tempted to linger, enjoying the colourful stalls, the cheerful shouts of the market traders. But it started to rain and reluctantly she turned her steps back towards Warwick Square, head bent against the wind.

She looked up when a carriage rolled to a stop beside her and someone called out, 'Get in - quickly,'

It was Mister Oliver. He opened the door and leaned out. 'Come along – you're getting wet.' He smiled, reaching out a hand to help her inside.

She gasped as he grasped her arm and pulled her inside, calling up to the coachman to drive on.

'We'll soon have you home and in the warm,' he said, smiling. 'Can't have a pretty little thing like you catching cold, can we?'

She smiled back tentatively, shivering. He unfolded a warm woollen rug from the seat beside him and, leaning forward, wrapped it around her. He moved to sit beside her and took her hands, chafing them gently. 'It's Ruby, isn't it?'

She nodded. 'Yes, sir,' she whispered.

The carriage lurched as it went over a pothole in the road and she fell against him. He laughed and put his arm around her. 'That's better. Don't worry, you're safe with me.'

And she believed him. Even when he kissed her before letting her out of the carriage she thought he was just teasing. She ran across the mews and in at the side door, still feeling the imprint of his lips on hers.

Normally, she'd have shared the experience with Fanny. They'd often giggled together over her friend's infatuation with Archie Bass and Ruby's blushes at the sight of Constable Locker. But the encounter with Mister Oliver was different and Ruby told herself there would be no more kisses.

* * *

Most nights Ruby fell asleep as soon as she got into bed but tonight she lay awake listening to the snores of the two kitchen maids and going over the incident in the carriage. Had Mister Oliver just been kind, saving her from a soaking? But she remembered Annie's warning to keep out of his way and the whispers about the reasons for Prue and May's dismissal. Since coming to Exton House she had learned a lot and she was no longer the naive girl who had left the Foundling Hospital knowing nothing of the ways of the gentry.

Well, she wouldn't be taken in by his smiles and soft words she decided, turning over and pulling the blanket over her shoulders. Just as she was drifting off to sleep, she heard a sound and started up in bed. But, even as the door opened and Oliver crept into the room, his finger on his lips, eyes alight with mischief, she wasn't afraid. His gentle kiss in the carriage and his concern lest she should catch cold lulled her apprehension.

'Hush! Don't be alarmed. I just wanted to make sure you hadn't taken cold after that soaking,' he whispered.

She shook her head. 'I'm all right, sir.'

He came and sat on the side of the bed, putting his hand on her forehead. 'No fever,' he murmured. 'That's good.' His hand moved down to stroke her cheek, then her neck, lower still, reaching for her breast.

Her body went rigid and she tried to push his hand away.

'I'm not going to hurt you,' he said, his voice harsher now, as he tugged at the ribbons holding the neck of her nightgown closed. She moaned in protest and he put his free hand over her mouth. 'Quiet. I said I won't hurt you.'

Now she was terrified but she daren't cry out and disturb the other maids. They would never believe that she had not encouraged him. And if Mrs Catchpole found out, it would mean instant dismissal.

She fought him as best she could, managing to find the strength to hit out. She must have hurt him and she gave a satisfied smile as he groaned and hissed, 'You'll pay for that, you little bitch.'

Just then Kitty sat up and called out in a frightened voice, 'Who's there?'

With a muttered oath Oliver scrambled away and made for the door, but not before he had whispered harshly, 'I'll be back.'

* * *

Every night after that, she lay awake, dreading his return. But he didn't come up to the attic again and she hoped that the presence of the two kitchen maids was keeping him away. It didn't stop him making threats though, and he would corner her in the linen cupboard or the upstairs corridor and pin her against the wall, fondling her and whispering about what he would like to do to her when he got the chance.

From then on she tried to make sure that one of the other maids was always with her when she went to tend the fires or change the beds. On the days she waited at table he would brush his hand against her as if by accident, the action accompanied by a sly smile.

She was just beginning to feel safe when he came to her room again. This time his assault on her body was brutal. She tried to cry out but he kept his hand over her mouth so that she could hardly breathe. All the while he whispered vile words in her ear. How on earth had the two kitchen maids slept through it, she wondered when at last it was over. He paused by the door, looking down at her with a smirk. 'I'm off to Yorkshire in the morning. I don't suppose you'll miss me, will you?' He laughed. 'Well, I won't miss you – there are plenty of pretty girls in Yorkshire. I won't go short.'

The next day Mr Phelps announced that Mister Oliver was off to visit friends at Brampton Hall in Yorkshire. 'He and the Bramptons will be back just before Christmas,' he said.

'Visitors,' Mrs Andrews muttered. 'More work.'

'It is not for us to question our betters,' Mr Phelps said.

Ruby only wished the master's son would stay away for ever. But she sighed with relief that she would at least have a respite from his attentions. Her relief that her torment was at an end was so great that she began to regain her old zest for life; to enjoy the laughter and banter round the big table in the basement kitchen. And with Mrs Catchpole disappearing for hours at a time to visit her sick sister, the servants were able to laugh and gossip as they worked without the fear of her acid-tongued reprimands.

* * *

For Ruby, the respite did not last long. Not only was Oliver due back any day, but on several mornings just lately she had woken up feeling nauseous, hardly able get out of bed. She felt a bit better after she'd been sick but she was terrified. Kitty had explained that the sickness was how they'd known what was wrong with Prue. If anyone suspected that she was suffering the same fate, she knew what would happen. Luckily no one seemed to have noticed anything - for the moment anyway.

She was cracking eggs into a bowl and separating the yolks as Mrs Andrews had showed her, trying to ignore the nausea which assailed her most mornings just lately.

When Hetty Catchpole came into the kitchen, she concentrated on her work, anxious not to catch her eye. She was sure that the housekeeper would guess what was wrong with her.

She looked up sharply when Mrs Catchpole addressed her. 'Pay attention, girl. I'm talking to you. You're to go up and help Fanny with the linen.'

Mrs Andrews looked up, her eyes blazing. 'Now look here, Mrs Catchpole. How am I supposed to manage if Ruby's working upstairs? I've got too much to do as it is – you know we've got visitors arriving any day now.'

'You've got Kitty and Annie. You'll just have to make the best of it, won't you?'

'It's about time we had a new housemaid.'

'I interviewed a girl last week but she wasn't suitable. We're managing, aren't we?'

Ruby kept her head bent during this exchange and carried on cracking the eggs. Nice as it would be to have a change of scene and spend time with her friend, she hated working under the housekeeper and bearing the brunt of her sharp tongue.

'Come along then, girl. I haven't got all day,' Mrs Catchpole snapped.

With a frightened glance at Mrs Andrews, Ruby wiped her hands on a cloth and followed the housekeeper out of the kitchen.

'You can have her back when she's finished,' Mrs Catchpole said.

'Well, don't keep her too long,' the cook replied, muttering under her breath as she went back to her pastry-making.'

Ruby hurried up the stairs, her legs already aching as she climbed two flights of stairs and hurried along the corridor to the linen closet at the end of the passage. Would they ever get a new maid or would she have to do two people's work from now on?

'Fanny will show you what to do – and don't take too long about it or I'll have Mrs Andrews complaining.' With a swish of her skirt and a jingle of the keys at her waist, the housekeeper left them to it.

Fanny smiled at Ruby and said, 'Nice to have your help. I've been struggling a bit on my own.' Her eyes welled with tears. 'Poor Prue – I do miss her.' She dashed a hand across her face and attempted a smile. 'Now, help me to get these sheets down from the shelf and then we've to take them to the guest rooms and make up the beds.'

Taking the pile of sheets from the shelf, she followed Fanny along to the main guest room where the Bramptons were going to sleep.

They worked in silence for a few minutes and, as they spread the counterpane over the freshly made bed, Fanny looked up and gave Ruby a sharp look. 'You're very quiet; you sure you're all right?' she asked.

'I'm fine. Come on, let's get this finished.'

Ruby was sorry she'd snapped but the tension was making her irritable. Thanks to Kitty's gossiping, she knew what Prue had done to get sent away. But Fanny didn't seem as outraged as the other servants. Perhaps she could confide in her but what good would that do?

It wasn't the poor girl's fault, as Ruby now knew. Still, in her short time here, she had learned that those below stairs would always be blamed for anything that went wrong. And now it seemed it had happened to her too. Perhaps she should confide in her friend, although she couldn't bear the thought that Fanny might think she had encouraged the master's son.

But how could she stop him? When he arrived back from Yorkshire she knew that he would not leave her alone – at least until her condition became obvious and she was thrown out. And what would happen to her then? Her eyes welled with tears and she scooped up the dust sheets and hurried out of the room, hoping that she would have herself under control by the time Fanny caught up with her.

Her friend seemed to sense that there was something wrong and, as they started preparing the room for the Honourable Amelia, the Bramptons' daughter, she kept up a flow of chatter about Archie and where they were going on their next day off.

'That's if we ever manage to get time off with all this extra work,' she said, smoothing the counterpane. She gave a quick look round the room and, satisfied that all was done according to Mrs Catchpole's strict standards, she smiled and said, 'Time for our dinner, Ruby.'

Although she had no appetite, Ruby followed her downstairs and went into the kitchen where the rest of the servants were already seated around the big table. Her stomach heaved at the smell of the stew Mrs Andrews was doling out but she forced herself to eat a little if only to stave off any comments about her health.

They were just finishing when Mr Phelps banged the handle of his knife on the table and called for silence.

'As you all know, the master's friends are arriving tomorrow and staying for two weeks. Mister Oliver is travelling with them. They will be coming by train and Williams will fetch them from the station.'

'How many extra will I be feeding' Mrs Andrews asked.

'Just the Bramptons and their daughter, the Honourable Amelia – and her maid of course.'

'The rooms are all ready,' Mrs Catchpole said. 'Well, I hope so.' She turned to Fanny and Ruby. 'I will be up to inspect them this afternoon.' She stood up.

'Just one moment, Mrs Catchpole. I have an announcement to make,' said Mr Phelps. 'I have been informed that Mister Oliver is to marry Lady Amelia Brampton. He will announce their engagement tonight.'

'Married, eh?' Mrs Andrews said. 'Perhaps that will put a stop to his carryings-on – but I doubt it.'

Mr Phelps gave her a stern glance and came out with his usual pompous remark. 'It is not for us to question the ways of our masters,' he said.

'When is the wedding?' Ruby asked eagerly. Perhaps Mrs Andrews was right and

Oliver would leave her alone once he was married. A foolish thought, probably. Marriage didn't stop someone like Oliver Preston from dallying with servant girls.

'None of your business, girl,' Mrs Catchpole snapped. 'Now back to work everyone.'

'I hope you don't need Ruby this afternoon,' Mrs Andrews said. 'I have plenty for her to do down here with all this extra food to prepare.'

'Very well,' the housekeeper said.

As they returned to work, Annie and Kitty chattered excitedly about the forthcoming engagement but Ruby didn't join in. She couldn't stop thinking about Oliver and trembling at the thought of him coming to her room. Could she tell him about the baby? And would it stop him assaulting her? It was more likely he would make sure she was turned out without a character like poor Prue?

Chapter Four

Ruby was worn out what with having to do two people's work, not to mention trying to keep Mrs Andrews and the housekeeper happy, as well as feeling so ill. The two women were constantly at loggerheads as to who had the claim on her time. In addition to this, the whole house was in an uproar with the extra work caused by the Prestons' guests.

She didn't mind too much as she and Fanny and had become good friends. She'd never had a special friend before except for Mary and that hadn't lasted long. She had been sent away to work in the shoe factory and Ruby had missed her terribly. But relationships were not encouraged in the Foundling Hospital and there was always the knowledge that when they left they could be sent far away and never see those they had grown up with again. How she envied Fanny living with her parents and two young brothers in their quarters over the coach house. The boys helped with the horses when they weren't at school and Mrs Williams did the laundry and gave a hand in the big house when the family was entertaining.

If only she had a family too, Ruby thought. Still, despite having to work so hard and being constantly tired, she had been happy here – at least she had until recently. Sir Charles and Lady Anne were good employers, treating their servants well with reasonably comfortable quarters and good food. She'd have been pleased to stay here forever, if it were not for Mister Oliver and the trouble she was now in.

Apart from the Foundling Hospital and those few barely-remembered years with her foster mother, Exton House was the only home she had ever known. But for how much longer, she wondered.

In her short time here, Ruby had learned a lot, mainly from listening to Kitty and Annie gossiping about the other servants. She had been shocked when she learned why Prue had been dismissed and, especially the whispers about who had been responsible. She hadn't really believed it until it happened to her.

As they dusted and polished the furniture and carried cans of hot water up and down the stairs, she scarcely listened to Fanny's chatter, working mechanically as she thought back to that dreadful day, a few short months ago.

They were tidying the mistress's room after her bath and while Fanny gathered up the soiled linen, Ruby got on with the dusting.

She replaced the ornaments she had taken from the windowsill, first making sure there was not a speck of dust on them. The housekeeper had very keen eyesight and would make her do the work all over again if it did not come up to her exacting standards.

Satisfied, she straightened the heavy brocade curtain and was about to turn away when she spotted movement in the mews below.

She shrank back, thinking it was the master's son. She couldn't bear the sight of him. But as she realized who it was, she couldn't stop a smile from curving her lips.

'Fanny, that policeman's there again' she said. 'I wonder what he wants.'

'He often stops for a chat with my dad when he passes on his beat.'

'Kitty says he only stops by so that he can see you,' Ruby said.

Fanny laughed. 'She's wrong about that. Besides, I'm practically engaged to Archie.'

It was a bright sunny day and, despite the cold, Ruby lingered at the window, wondering what the two men were talking about.

'The day I arrived here, he told Mrs Catchpole he was looking into a burglary but that was months ago,' she said. 'I wonder if they were ever caught.'

'No. My dad says there have been lots more break-ins. Constable Locker is determined to catch them but the gang is very clever.'

'It's frightening to think of someone getting into the house while we're asleep,' Ruby said.

'I'm not scared now that Archie's here - he's sworn to defend me,' Fanny said with a laugh.

The policeman was still talking to Mr Williams but suddenly he turned and looked up at the window where Ruby was standing. He had taken off his tall hat and the sun gleamed on his thick golden hair. He must have spotted her at the window and he smiled and gave a little bow.

Without thinking about it she smiled back and raised her hand. A strange feeling came over her and caught her breath.

'Ruby, stop day-dreaming.' Fanny's voice broke into her chaotic thoughts and she turned away, telling herself not to be so silly.

She picked up the polish and dusters – just in time as Mrs Catchpole appeared in the doorway.

'Come along you two, haven't you finished yet? There's a lot to do this morning.' At the housekeeper's sharp voice, Ruby hastily smothered her smile.

'We're just going,' Fanny said, indicating her armful of sheets. 'I'm just taking these down to the laundry.'

'Get a move on then,' Mrs Catchpole snapped. 'And no gossiping.'

As she turned away, Ruby summoned up her courage and spoke up. 'When is the new maid coming, Mrs Catchpole?' she asked.

'Not until next week, meanwhile, you'll just have to manage. I don't know what you're complaining about, Ruby Hinton. I should think you'd be glad to get out of the kitchen for a while.'

'Oh, yes, Mrs Catchpole. I am, thank you.'

'Well then.' The housekeeper left the room and hurried downstairs. As the girls followed her, Fanny whispered, 'I saw you blushing when we were talking about Constable Locker,' she said. 'He is rather good-looking, isn't he?'

Ruby shrugged. 'I don't know what you mean,' she protested.

Fanny giggled and was about to say something else but Ruby dismissed her teasing and said, 'We ought to get on in case Mrs Catchpole comes back to check on us.'

She didn't want to admit that she was attracted to the young policeman and had started to look out for him on his patrols past the house. What was the use after what had happened? Nothing could possibly come of it now.

She hoped Fanny would drop the subject and to her relief, she seemed to sense her embarrassment. 'Don't take too much notice of Mrs C,' she said. 'She's always like this when we have guests. She knows that if everything isn't just so, she's the one in trouble. It's her job to make sure everything's done properly.'

'Well, I just hope things will get easier when the new maid comes. I haven't been feeling too good lately,' Ruby said.

'Perhaps you've got a touch of the flu,' Fanny said sympathetically. 'My little brother hasn't been well either.'

Ruby didn't answer. It definitely wasn't the flu which was making her sick and she almost blurted it out to Fanny. But her friend couldn't help. No one could. She would end up in the workhouse. That would be worse than the Foundling Hospital.

Chapter Five

Swinging her basket on her arm, Ruby wandered through the market looking at the stalls. Even on a grey chilly day like today, it was a treat to be outdoors. She never minded when Mrs Andrews sent her on an errand and, although she knew she'd be in trouble if she didn't hurry back, she couldn't resist the temptation to linger.

The sickness she had been suffering from lately seemed to have eased off and she had dared to hope that her fears had been groundless. But as she had dressed this morning, her thickening waistline as well as the swelling of her breasts, told her that she was truly with child. How long before Annie and Kitty noticed and made some remark, she wondered.

Now, as she completed her errand for the cook, she tried to put it out of her mind and enjoy these few minutes' of freedom from the demands of Mrs Andrews and Hetty Catchpole. One or other of them was always on at her. As fast as she finished one job it was on to the next with scarcely time to take a breath.

She passed the pie stall and inhaled the aroma of rich gravy and warm pastry. For the first time in weeks, the smell didn't make her feel sick and she realized she was hungry. Her mouth began to water and she wished she hadn't spent her last penny on that juicy red apple. A pie would have been more filling. She'd been saving the apple to share with Fanny. Although the servants were reasonably well-fed at Exton House, it was a real treat to have a whole piece of fruit all to herself.

It was no good, she had to eat it now. Fanny would never know, she told herself. But as she lifted it to her mouth to take a bite, a pang of guilt assailed her. She remembered all the times Fanny had shared titbits with her. Her mother was a good cook and she often saved a piece of pie or a scone for her friend.

Now Ruby ruefully rubbed the apple on her sleeve and was about to replace it in the cloth bag which hung at her waist when a hand tugged at her skirt and a voice piped. 'Ain't yer gonna eat it then, miss?'

She looked down at a small boy whose rags scarcely covered his skinny frame. Stick thin legs poked from beneath ragged breeches and he shivered in the chill air. But it was the eyes, huge in the peaky face, which stopped her from pushing him away. Yes, she was hungry, but this poor child looked half-starved. At least she would be getting supper tonight but who knew when he'd get the chance to eat again. Without stopping to think she held the apple out to him.

'You have it.' The words were hardly out of her mouth before he had snatched the fruit and scampered off to disappear into the crowds thronging the market place. Ruby smiled and turned away. She had finished Mrs Andrews's errands and really ought to be on her way.

As she threaded her way between the stalls she caught another tantalising whiff from the pie stall. Perhaps she should have bought a pie after all. That would have filled the lad's belly far better than an apple, she thought. She sighed. There were far too many of these waifs and strays on the streets of London. Not all were as fortunate as she had been to be brought up in the Foundling Hospital. It had been drummed into her from a very early age that she must count her blessings. And she did. She knew all too well that she could have ended up like that poor little boy, scavenging the streets for something to fill his belly. She could have could have ended up in the workhouse or been abandoned in the street, perhaps dumped in a baby farm where she would have been neglected and abused, or even thrown in the Thames like so many unwanted babies.

As she left the busy market and turned into a quiet street she heard a raucous voice from behind her shouting, 'Stop, thief.'

She recognised the lad straight away as he raced past her, hotly pursued by a brawny stall holder and a constable.

The policeman caught him first, picking him up by the collar and shaking him. The half-eaten apple fell out of his hand and rolled into the gutter. 'Now then, lad. What do you have to say for yourself?' he said.

'Stole it, he did. Off my stall. Thieving little varmint,' the stallholder interrupted, making a grab for the boy.

'Hold on, sir. Did you see him take it?'

Before the stallholder could reply Ruby came up to them. 'He didn't steal it. I gave it to him,' she said.

The boy nodded vigorously. 'That's right, sir. The lady give it me.'

The stallholder laughed. 'A likely story,' he said, looking Ruby up and down, a sneer on his face.

She could tell what he was thinking. In her long black dress and mob cap, a shawl round her shoulders, she certainly couldn't be described as a lady. He probably thought she and the lad were working the market together.

The policeman, who still had a tight grip on the lad's collar, turned to Ruby. 'Did you really give it to him or are you trying to protect him?' he asked.

Ruby blushed as she recognized Constable Locker. He smiled kindly and she hoped he'd believe her when she said, 'He looked hungry, sir. Besides, I have a dinner waiting for me when I get home.'

The policeman addressed the stallholder. 'I asked if you actually saw him take it.'

'Well, he's been hanging around the market all morning. And when he walked past, munching on one of my apples, bold as brass, what else could I think?' The man was blustering now. 'Anyway, how do I know the two of them aren't in it together?'

'I don't think so. This young lady is a maid at Exton House, employed by Sir Charles

Preston – a respectable household. Unless you can swear you saw the boy thieving, I'll have to let him go.'

The lad, who'd been squirming in the constable's grip, tears streaking his dirty face, looked up hopefully. 'Please, mister. The lady's telling the truth,' he said.

The stallholder shrugged. 'I suppose that's that then. But somebody should pay for the fruit.'

Ruby stamped her foot. 'You're just trying it on, you are. I paid for that apple fair and square and I gave it to the lad.'

'All right, all right.' He turned to the boy, waving a threatening fist in his face. 'Well, don't let me see you near my stall again, that's all.' He stomped off, still muttering.

The policeman let go of the boy's collar and he scampered away, pausing to scoop up the half-eaten apple from the gutter. 'Ta, miss, sir,' he said and disappeared round the corner.

'I thought you were going to arrest him – and me,' Ruby said.

Constable Locker laughed. 'He's probably eaten the evidence by now.'

'How did you know where I worked?' Ruby asked him, although she knew he'd noticed her. He'd given her that little wave the other day when he spotted her looking out of the window.

'I pass Exton House regularly on my beat. I've often seen you coming and going on errands,' he said.

Ruby felt a blush creeping up her cheeks but she couldn't admit that she'd recognized him too. He seemed to spend a lot of time hanging around Warwick Square and she'd assumed he was walking out with a servant in one of the neighbouring houses. She covered her confusion with a gasp. 'I must get back. Mrs Andrews will kill me – I've been gone far too long.'

'I'll walk along with you, if I may.' Ruby saw that he too was blushing. 'I ought to introduce myself - Constable Jeremiah Locker, at your service, ma'am, but you can call me Jerry.' He gave a mock bow and Ruby couldn't help laughing.

'I'm Ruby Hinton, housemaid at Exton House, as you know.'

'I saw you the day you arrived. You looked so scared.'

Ruby bit her lip and didn't reply.

'I take it you've settled in then? And they treat you well?

'Yes,' she whispered. 'It's all right.' How could she tell him the truth?

They walked along in silence for a few moments and Ruby stole a glance at him. He was tall, as all policemen were, very smart in his dark blue coat with the silver buttons and his tall hat. Blue eyes twinkled in a ruddy face which lacked the pallor of most Londoners.

His voice had a soft country burr and she guessed he had not lived in London for very long. Her heart skipped a beat as he smiled down at her and she found herself wanting to know more about him, but she knew that once he found out about her situation he would not want to speak to her again.

Hard as it was, she knew she should not encourage him and it was a relief when they reached the corner of Warwick Square. She said a hurried goodbye and, before he could reply, ran down the area steps and through the basement storerooms to the big kitchen at the back of the house.

As she burst through the door, Mrs Andrews advanced on her, waving a wooden spoon threateningly in her face. 'Where on earth have you been, girl? I've been waiting on those onions this past hour.' She grabbed the basket and gave Ruby a push. 'Get on up those stairs. Mrs Catchpole is on the warpath and young Fanny has been struggling to get the rooms done on her own.'

'I'm sorry, Mrs Andrews. It wasn't my fault.' Ruby started to explain but the wooden spoon came down on her arm with a loud thwack.

'I said get upstairs, girl.'

Smarting from the blow, Ruby ran up the back stairs and found Fanny struggling to fold a dust sheet by herself.

While the family had been away in Scotland those servants left behind had cleaned the house thoroughly from top to bottom – everything had to be spick and span, ready for the family's return. The chandeliers had been lifted down and their crystals washed and dried, the furniture polished to mirror-like perfection and the carpets rolled up and taken outside to be beaten until not a speck of dust or fluff remained.

Now that they were expecting visitors it all had to be done again. It had been easier when the Prestons were away as the servants could move about freely without having to make themselves invisible. Their employers thought that the only time a maid should be seen at her work was when she was summoned to fetch something. Now they were trying to move around the house without causing too much disruption and disturbing their masters.

Ruby helped Fanny to fold the dust sheet and looked round the room with satisfaction. Surely Mrs Catchpole would find no fault with their work this time?

'I'm sorry I left you so long. I had a bit of an adventure.'

Fanny's eyes widened. 'What happened?'

'I thought I was going to be arrested,' she said, smiling at the shock on her friend's face. She hastened to reassure her that she'd done nothing wrong and went on to tell her about giving the apple to the starving boy. 'I was going to share it with you but he looked so hungry.'

'You're too soft,' Fanny said. 'He probably would have stolen something if you hadn't given it to him.'

'That's what Jeremiah – Constable Locker – said.'

'Ooh, Jeremiah, is it?' Fanny teased.

Ruby blushed. 'You know him – he's the one who's friendly with your dad. He was very kind – to the boy,' she added hastily.

Fanny giggled. 'You'll be courting next.'

If only that were true, Ruby thought. But here was little chance of that now, even if he was interested in her. Unconsciously, she ran her hand over the barely perceptible swell of her stomach.

Fanny was about to say something else when the door opened and Mrs Catchpole came in. 'Haven't you finished yet?' she snapped. 'What took you so long?'

Ruby was a little afraid of the housekeeper who, although she didn't lash out as Mrs Andrews did, could still reduce the maids to tears with her cutting sarcasm. She was brave enough to speak up though. 'Fanny's had to manage on her own today. Mrs Andrews sent me on an errand and it took longer than I thought.'

Hetty Catchpole's lips thinned. 'She has no right to give you orders. I can't have you wandering off to the market when there's such a lot to get through.'

She went out, slamming the door behind her and Fanny giggled. 'Poor old Mrs Andrews is in for it now. Mrs Catchpole's been in a right mood lately – worse than usual.'

The girls made sure everything was tidy and went downstairs. Fanny said 'goodbye' and ran across the cobbled stable yard to have her dinner while Ruby entered the kitchen. The tantalising aroma of mutton stew greeted her and her mouth watered as Mrs Andrews ladled rich gravy and dumplings onto the plates. As she passed the plates round, the cook reminded them, as she often did, that they were lucky to have a place where they got three meals a day.

After being off her food the past few weeks, Ruby had got her appetite back but she found herself thinking of the ragged urchin in the market. She was glad it had been Constable Locker who'd caught him. She doubted that another policeman would have taken her word. As the servants silently devoured their food, she wondered dreamily if she'd see him again, starting as Mrs Catchpole rapped on the table and ordered them back to work. As she stood up and made her way through to the scullery with a pile of dirty crockery, she felt a twinge in her back. The pain had been at the edge of her consciousness all day, but the encounter with Jeremiah had put it out of her mind. Now, she was reminded of her situation and her spirits fell at the thought of what the future held.

Chapter Six

The next day a new face appeared in the kitchen. 'This is the new housemaid,' Mrs Catchpole announced, pushing forward a young woman who seemed much older than the other maids.

'Her name's Polly. She's a well-trained maid, worked for a friend of Lady Anne.'

'So why did she leave?' Mrs Andrews asked.

'Her lady died.' Mrs Catchpole turned to Fanny. 'You'll have to show her what to do. And you, Ruby, will be back in the kitchen.'

Ruby was sorry she would not be working with Fanny now, although she got on well enough with Kitty and Annie. But an extra pair of hands was very welcome and might put the cook and housekeeper in a better mood now.

She smiled at the new girl but there was no time to speak as Mrs Catchpole hustled her out of the kitchen saying that the drawing room still needed seeing to while the family was at breakfast.

She and Kitty were sent to scrub pans in the scullery and as they worked, the other maid kept up a constant flow of chatter about the new maid. But Ruby scarcely listened. Although the work in the kitchen was harder and she would miss Fanny, she was pleased that there was more chance of her being sent on an errand –

and being out of the house meant more chance to see Jerry.

Lost in thought, she started when the door burst open and Annie came in. Her face was flushed and her cap awry. Gasping for breath, she said, 'You're to come quick, Mr Phelps says.'

'What's happened?'

'What's wrong?'

The two girls spoke in unison.

'There's two policemen here. They want to question the servants.'

Ruby's heart began to beat faster. Excitement mingled with apprehension. Something dreadful must have happened to bring the police to the house but excitement won. Chiding herself for her foolish thoughts, she couldn't help hoping that Jeremiah was one of the policemen.

Downstairs, the servants were assembled in the big basement kitchen. Jimmy, the boot boy, looked frightened, but the kitchen maids were whispering together excitedly. Silas James, the footman, leaned against the dresser, examining his fingernails and looking bored. Cook sat at the head of the table, her normally ruddy complexion pale.

Mr Phelps shook his head, a worried expression ceasing his face. 'I do think they should have sought permission from Sir Charles before questioning us,' he said.

'That sergeant said it was urgent,' Mrs Andrews said. 'And goodness knows when the master will get back from his club.'

'I suppose it will be all right,' Mr Phelps said, but he looked doubtful.

The door to the housekeeper's sitting room opened suddenly and Hetty Catchpole came out, her face flushed. 'They want Ruby next,' she said.

Ruby couldn't seem to make her feet move and the housekeeper gestured impatiently. 'Go on, girl, they won't bite you.'

She entered the small room and stood just inside the door. The big red-faced man seated in Mrs Catchpole's chair smiled and beckoned her forward. 'Don't be alarmed, miss. Just a few questions. I'm Sergeant Harris and this is Constable Locker.'

Ruby felt the blush flooding her cheeks as he indicated the young man standing to one side. Although he smiled warmly at her, he did not indicate that they were already acquainted.

'Nothing to worry about, miss,' he said. 'Just tell the sergeant your name and then answer his questions truthfully.'

'I'm Ruby Hinton, sir,' she stammered.

'And how long have you worked here?'

'Six months or thereabouts.'

'What do you do on your days off; where do you go?'

'Nowhere,sir. Leastwise I don't have any family to visit and no friends apart from the people here. I sometimes go to the market to look at the stalls.' Her voice faltered and her legs began to tremble as she remembered the incident in the market. Had the stallholder accused her of stealing?

She glanced apprehensively at Jeremiah but the sergeant put her mind at rest. 'If you've done nothing wrong, you have nothing to fear. I just need to know if you've noticed anything unusual on your walks to and from the square.'

'What sort of thing?'

'Strangers hanging about, people who have no business in this area.'

Ruby shook her head. Then, emboldened by the realization that she was not suspected of anything, she said, 'Why are you asking, sir?'

Sergeant Harris glanced at the constable. 'There is no reason why we should not tell you. It will be common knowledge before long. There has been a very serious assault on a night watchman across the way. The poor man was employed to keep watch on the house belonging to the Armstrong family while they were visiting friends. A gang broke in to steal their valuables but the man interrupted them. They attacked him and he now lies gravely injured in the hospital.'

Ruby gasped. She didn't know the person they referred to but the thought of someone being so badly beaten horrified her. 'But how can I be of assistance, sir?' she asked.

Constable Locker smiled at her. 'It would be helpful if you stayed alert and reported anything out of the ordinary to us. You see, miss, this is not the first such incident. We believe that the gang may have an informer, someone who tells them when the owners are away from home and their houses empty.'

Ruby thought of her own employers and the fact that they had not been in residence when she arrived a few months ago. As Mrs Catchpole had said, their absence had brought about a certain slackness among the servants. Anyone watching the house would soon be aware of it. She spoke up confidently though. 'I am sure no one in this household would do such a thing. We are all grateful to have such a good master.'

Constable Locker hastened to put her mind at rest. 'Rest assured, no one in this household is under suspicion.'

After a few more questions the sergeant indicated that she was free to go and asked her to send Fanny in.

Back in the kitchen there was a buzz of speculation among the servants as to who the inside man might be. It was seldom that anything happened to break the monotony of their work and they were all rather excited.

Mrs Catchpole banged on the table for silence.

'I'm sure no one in this household had anything to do with it so why don't you stop gossiping and let the police do their job.'

Mrs Andrews sighed. 'Who'd have thought such a thing would happen here in Warwick

Square. It's a dreadful crime. Stealing is bad enough but to injure a defenceless old man…'

The kitchen maids gasped in horror at the reminder of the seriousness of the crime. 'Will he die?' Kitty asked.

'We must pray not,' said the cook. 'That would make it murder.'

There was another outburst and Mrs Catchpole stood up and clapped her hands. 'Now then, Mrs Andrews, no more idle talk. There is still work to be done.'

'You're right, Mrs Catchpole. Annie, get those potatoes peeled. And Kitty, have you finished scouring those pans yet?'

The kitchen maids scurried to do her bidding and she turned to Jimmy, the boot boy. 'I'm sure you've got plenty to do, too, lad.'

The boy got up and sulkily disappeared into the scullery.

Fanny came out of the housekeeper's room, followed by the constable. 'You may all return to your duties now,' he said.

As the two girls returned to their work, Ruby scarcely listened to Fanny's teasing about the handsome young constable. She was remembering Hetty Catchpole's reaction to seeing him outside the house on her first day here.

She remembered that while their employers were away, the housekeeper had often gone out at night – to visit her sick sister, she said. But the servants' gossip told a different story. Still, Ruby couldn't help thinking that the idea of

Hetty Catchpole, with her beady eyes and thin lips, having a gentleman friend was ridiculous. Could she have been meeting someone and passing on information? She had certainly looked nervous at the sight of the policeman that day and today, she had been even more snappy and irritable than usual.

Ruby shook her head in denial. It was a ridiculous ides. Mrs Catchpole was a harsh mistress – slave-driver, Fanny called her – and she had exacting standards, but she was a respectable servant in a respectable household.

Still, Constable Locker had asked if she'd noticed any unusual happenings lately and the housekeeper's frequent and surreptitious absences were certainly that. Perhaps she should have mentioned it but fear of the housekeeper's temper had kept her silent.

* * *

Oliver and the Bramptons were due to arrive any minute and Ruby had no time to dwell on the burglary or her suspicions of the housekeeper, still less to day dream about Constable Locker. They would be here in time for tea and there was still a lot to do. The rooms must be spick and span. Hot water must be brought up in heavy cans and soft towels laid out. Fires would have to be lit and warming pans placed in the beds, for although it was still early autumn there was a distinct chill in the air.

Even with the new maid to help, there was still a lot to do and Mrs Andrews had agreed that Ruby could be spared to work upstairs with Polly and Fanny.

As Ruby dusted the ornate gas globes and polished the brass pipes and taps once more, Fanny came in.

'That's one of my favourite jobs,' she said.

'This gas lighting is marvellous, isn't it?' Ruby replied.

'At least we don't still have to fill those smelly oil lamps,' Fanny agreed.

Polly, who was brushing the long velvet curtains, turned and said, 'MY other lady still had lamps and candles. It's much nicer here. Nicer having other servants to talk to as well.'

'Lots of houses in the square have gas now but we were the first. Lady Anne saw a demonstration at the Great Exhibition at the Crystal Palace and talked the master into it,' Fanny said.

'I wish he'd had it put in through the whole place. I hate going down to those store rooms with a candle or having to light a lamp.'

'Can't have everything I suppose,' said Fanny. 'And candles are fine for the likes of us.' She picked up the dusters and polish and said, 'Come on – time for our break.'

After making sure that no speck of dust remained to catch Hetty Catchpole's eagle eye, Ruby followed the other girls downstairs just as the grandfather clock in the downstairs hall chimed twelve.

When they entered the kitchen, Gladys was gossiping about Mister Oliver's forthcoming engagement and the other servants were hanging on her every word. Gladys had seen the Honourable Amelia Brampton when she was in Scotland and she knew more about the family's goings-on than anyone else.

'Her family's very rich – even richer than - .' She stopped speaking as the door was flung open and Hetty Catchpole stalked in. Two spots of colour flamed on her thin cheeks and her eyes glittered. 'I've spoken to her ladyship but she won't give in,' she announced.

'I could have told you not to waste your time,' Cook said.

'But she must realise we can't manage with the servants we've got. It's a bit easier now we've got Polly but when we have visitors we need extra staff. But her ladyship insists it's out of the question.'

'Mean old skinflint,' Jimmy muttered.

The butler looked up sharply and cuffed the boy round the head. 'Mind your manners, young man,' he said. 'Have some respect for your betters.'

Jimmy sniffed and bent his head to the plate of stew, his expression mutinous.

Cook intervened. 'It's not her – it's the master. Anyway, we can't do anything about it. We'll just have to manage, though gawd knows why they have to have a big engagement party here. The Honourable Amelia's parents have already laid on a lavish do up in Norfolk.'

'Her ladyship wants to impress all their London friends I suppose,' said Hetty.

'Will it be a long engagement?' Ruby asked.

'None of your business, girl,' Hetty snapped.

Ruby had only asked in the hope that the wedding would follow soon and that Oliver Preston would move out of her life.

Despite Hetty's disapproval, the servants continued to gossip about their employers. The rumour was that once married he would move to his new wife's home in Norfolk and take over the management of the Brampton Manor estate. It couldn't happen soon enough for Ruby.

'Her ladyship's relieved that he's settling down at last,' Mr Phelps said. 'And of course, with Miss Amelia being the only child – no sons to follow – he'll inherit the estate eventually.'

'What's she really like?' one of the kitchen maids asked.

'She's no beauty I admit, but she has a sweet smile,' said Mr Phelps. 'Quiet little thing. I expect that's why he chose her – that and her money.'

'Living up there in the country will put a stop to his goings-on,' Cook observed with a sniff. 'No more young man about town, gambling and suchlike, spending Sir Charles's money.'

'It's his sisters I feel sorry for. Let's hope they both make good matches before their brother brings scandal down on the family name,' said the butler.

As Ruby finished her stew she looked up and by chance caught Hetty Catchpole's eye. She felt herself blushing at the housekeeper's next words. 'I think that's most unlikely. He's sowed his wild oats and now that he's engaged, he'll knuckle down and do his duty.'

She seemed to be looking straight at Ruby and she hurriedly stood up and took her bowl to the sink, wondering how she'd get through the day if this pain didn't let up.

She hurried out of the room conscious of the housekeeper's beady eyes on her, knowing that she could not keep her condition secret for much longer. And if she did, what would she do when the baby came? If she was discovered, it would mean instant dismissal and a hasty despatch to the workhouse.

They scarcely had time to finish their meal before they heard the carriage outside. Silas leapt to his feet and rushed up the basement stairs to open the front door. The other servants followed and lined up in the front hall to welcome their guests. Ruby stood beside Fanny, holding her breath as Silas opened the front door just as Williams jumped down to open the carriage door.

Oliver Preston stepped out and stood looking around him for a moment before turning back to help an older couple out of the carriage, followed by a slim young woman. So this was the Honourable Amelia, Ruby thought, noting the girl's pallor. She didn't look too happy to be here but she could just be tired from the journey. Ruby felt a little sorry for her and wondered how much the girl really knew about her fiancé's true character. It was none of her business however and she knew that often these marriages were often business arrangements rather than love matches.

From the moment the guests arrived until they had all retired for the night, the servants were kept on their feet. Ruby was the last to go up, having been kept behind by the cook to get things ready for the morning.

Finally, Mrs Andrews let her go and she made her way wearily up the attic stairs, where an additional truckle bed had been installed in Polly's room for Miss Amelia's maid, Hodges. Kitty and Annie were still chattering excitedly about the forthcoming wedding but they stopped when Hodges came up the stairs, pausing at the door to the kitchen maids' room.

Her haughty manner had already annoyed Ruby who had done her best to be friendly and put the new girl at her ease. And she was relieved when the girl opened the opposite door without speaking to them.

The Bramptons had with them a valet as well as the ladies' maid. The valet would attend to Amelia's father and Hodges would look after her mistress and Lady Brampton.

When they had arrived, Mrs Catchpole had asked Ruby to show Hodges where she would be sleeping and to bring her downstairs for tea after she'd finished unpacking her mistress's clothes.

'I'll help if you like. You must be tired after that long journey,' Ruby said.

The other girl shrugged. 'I travel everywhere with Miss Amelia. We've been to London many times, even to Paris.'

'I'd like to travel,' Ruby said wistfully, knowing that it would probably never happen. She unfolded a silk negligee and held it up to the light, marvelling at its softness.

Hodges snatched it away. 'Don't touch that. Miss Amelia doesn't like anyone else to see to her clothes.'

Ruby was a bit taken aback at the maid's tone but she kept her voice friendly. 'Did Mrs Catchpole tell you that you'd be sharing a bedroom with Polly – she's the other housemaid?'

'It's not what I'm used to but it's only for a few days.' Hodges shrugged. 'Besides, I hardly expected a room to myself in a house this size,' she said with a hint of disdain. She finished folding her mistress's clothes and began setting out her toiletries on the dressing table. 'I had expected more servants. Mister Oliver doesn't even have his own valet. And his sisters even have to share their mother's maid.'

'Well, in a house this size, there's hardly room for more servants.' Ruby couldn't keep the hint of sarcasm out of her voice.

Hodges continued to boast about her mistress's establishment. 'We have proper bathrooms and gas light in all the rooms. You should see the chandeliers in the ballroom, brighter than the sunniest day.'

Ruby was moved to defend her employers. 'We have gas lighting too. Exton House was the first in this square.' When she'd first come here they had still been using oil lamps and candles. The servants had grumbled at the upheaval when the pipes and gas jets were installed but it was worth it. Ruby had been amazed at the difference it made. She had never seen gas candelabra before. And there was gas lighting in the kitchen too.

'But not in the whole house.' Hodges seemed to take pleasure in reminding her. 'I notice that the servants still have to carry candles up to their rooms.'

It was true and Ruby had sometimes wondered why. Silas had said it was just another example of their employer's meanness. She couldn't think of a suitable retort but she tried for one more attempt at friendliness. 'Why does your mistress call you Hodges? What's your first name?'

'At Brampton Hall all the maids are called by their surnames. It's the proper way.' She sniffed as if she did not approve of the way things were done at Exton House.

'How many servants are there?' Ruby asked.

'Many more than you have here. Brampton Hall is huge, fifteen bedrooms alone. Then there are the grounds and the farms. I hear Mister

Oliver is to manage the estate when he and my mistress are married.'

'I believe so,' said Ruby.

'I confess I was surprised when the engagement was announced. I had expected Miss Amelia to make a better match.'

'Perhaps they love each other.' Ruby did not really believe it but she was just trying to be friendly.

The other girl gave a short laugh. 'I don't think so. It is more of a business arrangement. Miss Amelia has a good dowry. Anyway it's not our business how our employers conduct themselves. I don't wish to talk about it.'

Ruby gave up any further attempts at conversation. She just hoped the Bramptons' stay wouldn't be a long one. But, as she showed the girl the way to the basement kitchen where the servants had gathered for tea she reflected that there was some consolation in having Hodges there. Nothing seemed to disturb the two kitchen maids and Ruby suspected that fear would make them pretend to be asleep if Mister Oliver tried to get in. But surely he wouldn't dare to try and enter while his fiancée's maid was sleeping just across the landing.

* * *

Ruby had finally managed to get some sleep, but it seemed only moments before Kitty was shaking her awake. With the extra people in the house, there was so much more to do. Hot water had to be carted up to the bedrooms, fires lit and breakfast served in the dining room. It was mid-morning before she was allowed to stop and have breakfast and by then the nagging pain in her back, which she had felt on and off for days, had returned.

She tried to hide her discomfort and bent her head over the bowl of porridge which Kitty put in front of her. Not that she felt like eating but she had to keep her strength up, she told herself.

She looked up as Mr Phelps came into the kitchen.

'The master is very angry that we allowed those two policemen in to question the servants,' he said. 'He should have been informed.'

'Your job I would have thought, Mr Phelps,' Mrs Catchpole said sharply.

'As you know, I was engaged upstairs and was not aware that they were here.'

'They were only doing their job,' said Mrs Andrews 'Just think - it could have been one of us knocked over the head instead of poor old Joe.'

'They say he's still unconscious and may not recover,' said Mr Phelps.

The kitchen maids' eyes grew round with horror and Jimmy gleefully increased their terror by saying, 'Perhaps we'll be next.'

Before Mr Phelps could reprimand him, Ruby said sharply, 'Stop it, Jimmy. You're talking nonsense. No one would dare to break in here while Sir Charles is at home. Besides, I'm sure the police are doing all they can to catch the burglars.'

She got up and busied herself at the sink hoping no one had noticed her quick blush as she spoke of the police. She had almost blurted out Constable Locker's name and that would have made her blush even more. She caught Fanny's eye and prayed that her friend wouldn't make one of her teasing remarks.

* * *

That night Ruby was just drifting off to sleep when Annie whispered hoarsely, 'Did you hear something?'

Kitty turned over and mumbled but Ruby sat up, heart thumping. But there was no sound from outside. Relieved, she said crossly, 'Annie, do be quiet. We're trying to sleep.' Annie seemed to have no trouble though, Ruby thought, listening to her snuffles and snores.

'Sorry, Ruby. I'm that nervous since we heard about poor old Joe,' the other maid said.

They were about to lie down again when the attic door opened.

Kitty gave a little scream which turned into a nervous laugh when she recognised Hodges. 'Oh, lawks, I thought it was a burglar.'

'Sorry – wrong door. My candle blew out,' Hodges said. 'I've only just finished seeing to Miss Amelia. You're lucky to be abed so soon.' She sniffed.

Ruby shrugged and forbore to point out that they would have to be up much earlier than the ladies' maid. 'Well, try not disturb Polly,' she said. 'And you, Kitty, don't worry – we're safe enough up here even if they do break in downstairs. Besides there's nothing in these attics worth stealing.'

'I still don't think I could sleep for worrying though,' Kitty said.

Ruby sighed impatiently but then she had an idea. Anything to get the other girl to settle down so they could all get some rest. 'If you're really frightened, we could push the chest against the door. No one could get in then.'

Ignoring Hodges's scoffing at their silliness, they got out of bed and pushed the heavy chest which contained their meagre belongings against the door. 'There,' said Ruby. 'We can do that every night until the burglars are caught.'

'I shall sleep easier now,' Kitty said, and Ruby nodded.

'Me too.' She wasn't afraid of burglars but now she had a good excuse for barring the door. Although she felt reasonably safe with Miss Amelia's maid close by, she would carry on doing so until Mister Oliver was safely married and away to Yorkshire.

As she drifted off to sleep she put a hand on her stomach. The sickness had passed and she had begun to hope that it had indeed merely been a touch of the flu. But as time went by she'd had to face up to the fact that she was in the same state as poor Prue who had been dismissed without a character and no place to go except the workhouse.

She couldn't stay here she thought, as she tossed and turned in her narrow bed. Could she get another job? She had no idea how to go about it. The authorities at the Foundling Hospital had arranged her employment with the Prestons. She did know that she'd have to have a reference from Lady Anne. And what reason could she give for wanting to leave? She certainly couldn't tell the truth.

She must have fallen asleep eventually but she felt as if she'd been awake all night as she fought free of the tangled blanket and put her feet on the cold bare floorboards. Her back ached and her eyes felt gritty and sore. And she still had no idea what she should do.

She stumbled over to the nightstand and poured cold water into the basin. After splashing her face and drying it on the rough towel she felt a little more wide awake. The kitchen maids were still yawning and stretching and she chivvied them to get dressed. With the speed of long practice they helped lace each others stays and pin up their long hair before creeping down the attic stairs to the big basement kitchen.

There would be little or no rest from now until the last of them had retired for the night once more and the servants were free to go to their own beds. Unlike some of the big houses, there were fewer servants than such a large household needed. Mrs Andrews declared that it was because of Sir Oliver's meanness but Mr Phelps had hinted at other reasons. To Ruby, the Prestons seemed extremely rich but after her conversation with Hodges she had learned that most upper class households had far more servants each with their own special duties.

Chapter Seven

Jeremiah was troubled. He walked along the street, shoulders back, his right hand on the truncheon which hung at his waist, eyes alert. He loved being a policeman and never regretted leaving his little Norfolk village to come to London. But there were aspects of the job which sometimes upset him, bringing back bad memories and sleepless nights.

Although the night watchman was now recovering from his injuries, Jeremiah was still angry about the attack and even angrier that so far they had not managed to arrest the culprits. Stealing was one thing, but a senseless attack on a defenceless old man was quite another. But they would catch the villains, he vowed, and they would be punished.

Catching criminals gave him great satisfaction – thieves, conmen, murderers abounded in the seething metropolis. Standing up in court and giving evidence held no terrors for him, despite the threats and intimidation from some of the more hardened criminals. They were either sent to jail or transported to the colonies where they could no longer hurt him.

Most respectable people thought that was what his job was all about. Sergeant Harris had told him that when the gentry first heard of the formation of the police force a little over thirty years ago, they were not in favour of the idea. But when they saw that their homes and property were protected they began to accept the sight of the constables in their smart uniforms patrolling the streets. There would always be crime and criminals but Jeremiah was proud to be doing his part to bring it down. But that wasn't all that his work entailed and it was this other aspect of his work that was troubling him today.

Besides the burglars, thieves and murderers that he was sworn to bring to justice, there was a disturbing undercurrent of crime that was more common than people realised, something going on which many hardly saw as a crime. And Jeremiah was determined to do his part in stamping it out.

Take this latest case, he thought. A poor little mite, wrapped in rags and thrown into the river. No one cared. Some poor ignorant girl, seduced probably, wanting to do the best for her illegitimate child and paying money she could ill afford so that she could comfort herself with the thought that it was being looked after by a kindly foster mother. She probably didn't even know her baby was dead and would carry on paying for years.

'Happens all the time. Baby farming they call it,' Sergeant Harris had said. 'Sounds innocent enough put like that,' he continued. 'Course, some of them are genuine baby minders. But most of them…' He paused, stroking his moustache.

'I didn't realise…' Jeremiah said.

'Well, there's no law against it, you see. Anyone can set up as a baby farmer and some people see it as an easy way to make money. But many of them don't care a fig for the children in their care. They're ill-treated, half-starved. And when they die, as they so often do, their bodies are disposed off like so much rubbish.' He sounded callous but Jeremiah knew the sergeant was just as upset as he was. He had just learned to hide his feelings better.

Jeremiah, however, could not hide his revulsion, although he told himself he should be used to it by now. His job had opened his eyes to all sorts of horrors.

'I hear there's a few in Parliament wants to put a stop to it, have them investigated, like, before they can set up in business,' the sergeant continued.

Jeremiah hoped the powers that be were successful and now, as his route took him past the Foundling Hospital, his heart lightened. There were people who cared, he thought. The place had been set up a hundred years ago by a rich sea captain wanting to do something for the hundreds of abandoned babies and children. Despite much opposition, he had enlisted the help of some famous people, among them the composer, Mr Handel. How sad that a hundred years later, despite the patronage of the famous writer, Charles Dickens, and other influential people, nothing seemed to have changed, Jeremiah thought. Ruby had been one the lucky ones. If it wasn't for those kind and charitable people he might never have met her.

He knew that most of the gentry refused to believe there was a problem. They thought the girls who got into trouble were loose women and deserved whatever happened to them. And their children, conceived in sin, were no better. He knew differently.

A lump came to his throat as the sweet innocent face of a young girl invaded his thoughts. She had been truly innocent until she'd gone to work at Thorleigh Hall where the squire was known for his lecherous ways. However poor they were, his parents should never have let her go there. His poor, sweet sister Daisy had come home in tears. In a way she was one of the luckier ones, having a family brave enough to face the shame and take her in. Not so lucky when the baby came though. The poor little mite had been still born and Daisy had slipped away soon after. Jeremiah, riven with grief, had tried to grab the shotgun which hung above the mantel in the cottage, declaring that he'd give the squire what he deserved. Fortunately, his father had managed to restrain him.

'Do you want us to lose the cottage, to see your mother in the workhouse?' Father raged.

His mother, sobbing, cried, 'He's not worth hanging for.'

Jeremiah had kicked a stool across the room and thrown himself down at the table, burying his face in his hands. 'I want justice for her,' he sobbed.

But there was no justice for people like them. The landowners and gentry held the power.

Unable to carry on working for the man he thought of as his sister's murderer, Jeremiah had left the village. He had tramped the thirty miles to Norwich in search of work. After a few weeks working in the shoe factory he had been ready to go back home. He'd been used to working outdoors and the cramped and noisy conditions of the huge workshop were almost unbearable. But his grief and anger hadn't lessened and he knew he could not return cap in hand to his old master in Thorleigh. Knowing what the man had done, Jeremiah wouldn't be able to stop himself taking revenge for his sister's death. It wouldn't help his parents if he was hanged or transported to Australia.

There was only one thing for it. He would join the army. But just as he was about to enlist, he spotted a handbill advertising for fit young men of good character to join the Metropolitan Police Force. The idea appealed to him. He might not be able to find justice for his dear sister, but perhaps in meting it out to others, he would find his salvation. After returning to Thorleigh one last time to say a heart-wrenching farewell to his parents he had set off for London.

He'd never regretted his decision despite sometimes missing the open fields and country lanes of his home county, the sweet smell of haymaking, the rowdy harvest suppers, the maypole on the village green.

London was a different world – a world of contrasts. There were the dark, foul-smelling lanes and alleys where the poor lived out their hopeless lives in cramped squalor. And then, just round the corner, as if you'd stepped over an invisible barrier, you would come upon the leafy squares surrounded by huge mansion houses where the gentry lived. Overall was the all-pervading fog, the choking smells of coal smoke and horse manure. Jeremiah soon got used it. Besides, he didn't mind the horsey smells – they reminded him of home.

He turned away from the mean streets and into Warwick Square where his beat ended. The contrast between the area he'd just left and this quiet square was overwhelming. It was hard to believe that only a few streets away, crowded shabby tenements were home to thousands, whole families crammed into single rooms, many of them on the verge of starvation, struggling to make a few coppers to feed their families. Crowded together in filthy narrow streets, disease was rife. And in such conditions crime flourished.

Jeremiah looked over the iron railings into the square's central garden, hoping he wouldn't catch sight of a vagrant sleeping in the shrubbery. He sometimes felt sorry for them having nowhere to go and hated having to run them off, but it was more than his job was worth to ignore them.

Relieved that today no one had sneaked into the private garden, he turned his attention to the big houses surrounding the square. Alert for anything out of the ordinary, he glanced down into the areas as he passed. The sight of a policeman patrolling on his regular beat was reassuring to the upper class inhabitants, especially after the recent spate of burglaries. The night watchman who'd been injured had at last recovered but the gang had not been deterred by narrowly escaping a murder charge. Another house in the square had been broken into a few days later and Jeremiah knew it would not be the last such incident.

Today, however, burglary was the last thing on his mind as he passed Exton House on the corner of the square. He was more interested in those below stairs, especially the little maid who worked there. Just one glimpse of Ruby Hinton with her chestnut curls and sweet smile was enough to brighten his day.

He'd often seen her as he walked his beat and had been longing for an opportunity to get to know her. He hadn't been able to believe his luck the other day when, after chasing the suspected thief, she had spoken up for the lad. If it had been anyone else he would have arrested them both. But, even if he hadn't recognised her, he would have been convinced of her innocence. He knew that some criminals –

confidence tricksters they were called – would use a pretty girl with an innocent smile to deflect suspicion. But Ruby had a good job in a respectable household. And it was only an apple, not the crown jewels, he told himself.

His liking for Ruby had been strengthened when he'd accompanied Sergeant Harris to Exton House to question the servants about the attack on the night watchman. She had not been afraid to answer his questions and had answered with a quiet directness. She hadn't burst into tears like the little scullery maid, or looked at him insolently as the housekeeper had.

Despite speaking to all the servants, no one had admitted knowing anything of course and Jeremiah knew that most were telling the truth. He had his suspicions though, which is why he spent so much time lately patrolling Warwick Square. At least that's what he told himself.

Now, as he walked past Exton House, he recalled Ruby's smile as he thanked her for her co-operation. That smile had been like a ray of sunshine in the gloomy room and since then he hadn't been able to get her out of his mind. Perhaps he would see her today, he thought, maybe get the chance to speak to her and get to know her better. He paused at the entrance to the mews in the faint hope that she would be crossing the yard or leaving the house on some errand.

There was no sign of her but he spotted a small boy crouched on the cobbles playing with a kitten. He looked up and saw Jeremiah, letting out a yell as he scurried into the nearby stable. A moment later Williams, the coachman, came out holding the boy by the hand.

'Something amiss, Constable?' he asked. 'Don't say there's been another burglary?'

'I'm afraid so. But I'm just on my regular beat today. I'm sorry if I frightened the boy,' Jeremiah said.

The boy tried to hide behind his father and Jeremiah crouched down and smiled. 'What's the kitten's name?'

A slow smile crept across the lad's face. 'He hasn't got one. Dad's going to drown them but he says we can keep this one.'

'He must have a name. He's a lovely colour. Why don't you call him Smoky?'

The boy nodded and looked up at his father.

'It's a good name, Alfie. Now, take him back to the stable and help your brother with the mucking out.' Williams turned to Jeremiah. 'He's supposed to be working, but he's a mite young yet. They grow up so fast, don't they?'

Jeremiah nodded. 'Does your wife work in the big house as well?'

'She does the laundry and helps out when needed, when there's guests and suchlike.' He paused. 'I believe you questioned my daughter, Fanny, the other day.'

Jeremiah nodded. 'I hope I didn't frighten her. Some people are nervous of the police. Not that I suspected anyone but my sergeant insisted we question all the servants.'

'You were just doing your job. And as I told Fanny and young Ruby, there's no reason to be nervous if you haven't done anything wrong.'

Jeremiah's heartbeat quickened at the mention of Ruby's name. He wanted to know more about her – was she walking out with anyone; did she get any time off? Stammering a little he said, 'My sergeant said much the same. I trust they – she – your daughter wasn't too distressed.'

Williams laughed. 'I think it's young Ruby Hinton you're really interested in. Have you taken a fancy to the girl?'

Jeremiah felt his face beginning to redden and Williams laughed again. 'Don't blame you, Constable. She's a lovely girl – least she was.'

'What do you mean?' Jeremiah's heart sank. What had happened to her?

'The girl's been right poorly – some sort of fever, I think. My Fanny said she was laid up for a couple of days and she's got very thin and pasty looking. Still, she must be on the mend, 'cause Fanny said she's back at work now.'

So that's why he hadn't seen her. Jeremiah sighed with relief. He became aware that the groom was staring at him, a smile on his lips and he pulled himself together. 'Better be on my way then,' he said.

As he turned away he glanced up and saw Ruby at an upstairs window. So she was better now, he thought, smiling. It was turning out to be a better day than he'd anticipated.

He must find a way to see her again, to get to know her better, despite the coachman's warnings about the housekeeper's strictness. With a half-salute, he walked off, whistling under his breath.

Chapter Eight

The house was in an uproar with preparations for the engagement party. Hetty Catchpole was more bad tempered than ever as she strode about the house, her eagle eye alert for the slightest speck of dust or a creased cushion.

The maids scurried around carting the china ornaments from the two rooms on the first floor down to the basement to be washed. Kitty and Annie, up to their elbows in soapy water, no longer giggled and chatted as they worked, nervous of breaking the precious porcelain vases and silver epergnes which usually graced the Regency sideboards.

The connecting doors had been pushed back to make one large room and Silas and Jimmy had rolled up the carpets ready for the dancing. Taking up the carpets had resulted in a fine film of dust over everything and Fanny and Ruby sneezed as they damped down the wooden floor before sweeping and polishing. The furniture had to be polished as well and the gilt handles and mirror surrounds cleaned with a fine feather duster. Since the arrival of the new maid Ruby had not been required to work upstairs so often and she had been missing the chance to chat with Fanny. In many ways though she was relieved to be free of the housekeeper's sharp tongue. Not today though.

She had been running a soft duster over the same surface for some minutes, lost in thought, when Fanny gave her a nudge. 'Wake up, Rube. Hetty's on the warpath.'

She started and began to polish the sideboard more vigorously. 'There, that should do,' she said, turning round as if she had only just realised the housekeeper had come into the room. 'Oh, Mrs Catchpole, we've finished in here. What would you like us to do now?'

Hetty sniffed and ran a finger over the wood panelling, giving a grim smile when it came away free of dust. 'Everything seems to be in order. Better get the other guest rooms ready. Miss Amelia's aunt and uncle arrive later on today. And you, Ruby, Mrs Andrews wants you back in the kitchen.'

As Ruby left the room she heard Fanny say, 'Please, Mrs Catchpole, may I go across to the stables and make sure my brothers are all right? Polly can manage without me for a few minutes.'

'No, you may not,' Hetty snapped. 'There's far too much to be done today.'

'But Mother's helping Cook in the kitchen and she doesn't like to leave them alone too long.'

'But your father's there. He can keep an eye on them. Now go and get the clean linen for the guest rooms.'

Ruby was waiting for her friend at the bend in the stairs and she gave a rueful smile. 'She's in a right mood,' she said.

'What's new?' Fanny replied. 'I know the boys are all right really. I was hoping to grab a bite of bread and cheese. The old besom hasn't let us have a break today.'

They went down the back stairs to the linen closet and Fanny filled her arms with fresh sheets and pillow cases. As Ruby went to carry on down to the basement, Fanny said, 'I wish you were still working with me. Polly's very nice but she's not easy to talk to.'

'I expect she's shy. She'll be all right once she's settled in.'

Ruby hurried down to the kitchen where Mrs Andrews was waiting impatiently. 'I thought now we have a new housemaid you wouldn't be needed upstairs,' she grumbled. 'Now, get on and fill those water jugs and take them up to the dining room.'

'Yes, Mrs Andrews,' Ruby said and hurried to do her bidding.

'And when you've done that, you need to help Kitty take up the hot water ready for when the guests arrive.'

Gladys, who always accompanied Lady Anne when the family went away, had boasted to the other servants that some of the houses they stayed in had proper bathrooms with hot water on tap.

Ruby wished she worked in a house like that. As she so often did, she found herself day-dreaming about getting another job, far away from Warwick Place and Oliver Preston. She was a hard worker and she was sure Lady Anne would give her a good reference. But how would she go about it? Most servants, she knew, stayed with the same family all their lives. Besides, this was the only home she had known since leaving the Foundling Hospital.

No use day-dreaming, she told herself, as she hurried back downstairs for the hot water cans.

Kitty had already taken one and Ruby followed. As she poured the hot water into the hip bath which stood in front of the fire, Kitty hurried back to the basement to fetch more for the other rooms. Ruby straightened her back to ease the ache which had been present for most of the day, sighed and turned to follow the other maid. As she reached the landing, the door opened and her face paled. Oliver lounged in the doorway, smirking. She took a step backwards, frantically looking around. But there was no escape. Even if she told him about the baby she knew he would just laugh and still expect to have his way with her.

His lips twisted in a cruel smile and he pushed her back into the room and closed the door. 'So, there you are, my dear. Thought I'd forgotten you? Well, here we are, alone at last. Did you miss me?' He laughed and seized her wrist, pulling her towards him.

'Please, sir, let me go,' she whimpered.

'No use making a fuss. There's no one on this floor. They're all downstairs in the dining room and your little friend won't be back either.' He pushed her backwards onto the bed and tore at her bodice.

Frantic, she tried to push him away. She wouldn't let it happen again, she just wouldn't. She kicked out at him and connected with his shin. He swore viciously but let go long enough for her to twist away. As she made for the door he rushed after her but his foot caught in the bed curtain and he fell against the chest of drawers. It delayed him long enough for her escape.

As she ran down the corridor, Mrs Catchpole appeared at the head of the stairs. 'What are you doing up here, girl? Get your clean apron on and go to the dining room at once.'

Thankful that the housekeeper hadn't seemed to notice her dishevelled hair and flushed face, Ruby hurried downstairs and changed her rough apron for a clean white one. Settling her cap on her head, she hurried along to the dining room to help Polly with serving luncheon.

As she stood against the wall, her hands folded demurely in front of her, waiting for a signal from the butler to begin serving, Oliver came into the room and took his place at table.

'I thought you were lunching at your club, Oliver,' Lady Anne said. 'Still, it's nice that you chose to join us, isn't it, Amelia?'

Oliver's fiancée smiled and a faint flush crept across her face.

He leaned across and took her hand. 'How could I keep away, my dear? The company of my fiancée is infinitely preferable to that of those old bores at the club.'

Ruby hid a cynical smile. Anyone would think he was desperately in love with the poor girl. How could she be taken in by him? If only she knew that the charming man sitting next to her hid a lustful monster behind his smile.

Miss Amelia was simpering up at him. 'We've had a delightful morning,' she said. 'Even at this time of year the parks are beautiful. And we met some of Oliver's friends while we were out.'

'So, you are enjoying your visit to London,' said Lady Anne.

'I must confess, I prefer the country, but London is a delightful city,' Amelia replied.

'The more delightful as you are here, my dear.'

Oliver's words brought another blush to Amelia's face.

Ruby felt she couldn't bear to listen to them a moment longer. But she had to stand there, her face impassive, pretending she could not hear the conversation. It occurred to her that Oliver was laying on the charm to his fiancée simply because he knew she was listening. She bit her lip, longing to flee the room.

As the Prestons and their guests continued with their meal, Ruby stole a glance at Fanny who had come in quietly with the dessert. Her friend seemed preoccupied and Ruby wondered what had upset her. Perhaps she was worried about her brothers.

At last Lady Anne signalled that they had finished eating and Mr Phelps chivvied the girls into clearing the dishes. As they loaded the trays with used crockery, Fanny whispered, 'Are you all right?'

Ruby nodded, although she was still shaken by her encounter with Oliver.

'Only I noticed you seemed upset when you came in.'

Ruby forced a smile. 'Mrs Catchpole's been on at me, as usual,' she said. There was no way she could tell her friend what had really happened.

But, as they reached the door to the kitchen, Fanny said, 'I wondered if Mr Oliver had been bothering you.'

Ruby hid her surprise. 'Why would you think that?' she asked.

'He grabbed me in the passage, tried to kiss me. Cheeky so and so – and him engaged to be married.'

'That wouldn't bother him,' Ruby said bitterly.

'Well, I know he has a reputation as a ladies' man. But I shoved him away and just as he went to grab me again, Mr Phelps came along. I've never been so pleased to see anyone in my life.' Fanny hefted the tray on her hip and took a deep breath. 'Anyway, he - Mister Oliver I mean – rushed away up the stairs. I knew you were up there and I wondered if he'd decided to try his luck with you.'

Ruby shook her head, still reluctant to confide in the other girl. She put her own tray down on a side table and went to open the kitchen door but Fanny stopped her. 'I'm sorry I didn't come to warn you. Mr Phelps nabbed me to go and help in the dining room.'

'It's all right. I'll make sure I keep out of his way though. And we'd better warn Polly as well.'

Later, as she said goodnight to Fanny and picked up her candle, she wondered if she should have told her friend that Mister Oliver did not stop at stolen kisses. But surely Fanny must know that he had already been responsible for the dismissal of two maids. It seemed that the master's son wasn't too particular who he vented his lust on. She couldn't bear the thought that her friend might suffer the same fate that she had. She couldn't tell her the whole story of course but it was only fair to warn her.

* * *

Jeremiah's beat today took him through the teeming streets of the poorer area nearer the river. As he strode along, alert for any signs of criminal activity, his thoughts kept straying to Ruby. He hadn't seen her for a while and he wished that Sergeant Harris would send him to Warwick Square again.

He should keep his mind on the job, he told himself, as a hawker with a tray of brightly coloured ribbons approached him.

'Buy a ribbon, sir? Lovely ribbons – buy one for your lady, sir.' He saw Jeremiah's hesitation and pressed him again.

Jeremiah shrugged. It was only a halfpenny. He picked a cherry red ribbon and folded it carefully into the breast pocket of his jacket. The next time he saw Ruby he'd find an excuse to speak to her. Once he'd assured her his intentions were honourable, he'd give it to her. He hoped it would be the first of many gifts to show his devotion.

He turned the corner into a narrow street of shops. Carriages and delivery carts rumbled over the cobbles, vendors shouted their wares, dogs barked. Above the mingled sounds Jeremiah heard the familiar cry, 'Stop, thief.'

Thoughts of Ruby fled as he unhooked the truncheon from his belt and gave pursuit. He soon spotted the thief, weaving in and out of the crowds, knocking over a pile of boxes balanced in the edge of the pavement. Leaping over them, Jeremiah soon caught up with the culprit, a skinny lad with white face and frightened eyes.

He looked very like the lad that Ruby had given the apple to. But he couldn't be sure. Besides, all these urchins looked alike. He shook the boy by the arm. 'Now then, what have you been up to, me lad,' He said.

'Weren't me, sir. I never done it,' the boy gasped.

'If you didn't steal anything, why did you run?'

'I were scared. He tried to grab me. But I never took nothing, sir.'

Jeremiah turned to the shopkeeper. 'Are you sure this was the lad?'

'Well, seeing as how he's got one of my pies in his pocket and he never handed over no money – yes, he's the one all right.'

'You'll have to come down to the station with me to make a statement.'

The shopkeeper began to protest about leaving his shop unattended but Jeremiah explained that without a witness statement he would be unable to detain the thief.

Keeping a firm hold of the boy's arm he marched him down to the police station, followed by the shopkeeper and a couple of bystanders who said they'd seen what had happened.

After making his own statement he handed the boy over to the sergeant and went on his way, feeling a little sad. He knew what was likely to happen to him and reflected that it was a pity there had been no Ruby this time to speak up for the thief.

Perhaps he was getting soft, he chided himself. In this job it was a major failing to try to see the best in everyone. But he couldn't help feeling sorry for these street urchins who, homeless and hungry, often had no recourse but to steal in order to survive. Then he recalled the contents of the deep pocket sewn into the lining of the boy's jacket. He knew that this time he'd done the right thing in arresting him. It was clear he was part of one of those gangs of street urchins who were sent out by their master to steal in return for food and a place to sleep.

Resuming his patrol of the teeming streets, Jeremiah felt a spurt of anger. If only they could catch the criminals who ran the gangs. But they managed to stay hidden and it was the children taken in by them who usually paid the price.

Resuming his patrol of the teeming streets, his thoughts went back to a disturbing case he had been involved in – the body fished out of the river a few days ago. His heart went out to the poor little mite, although he supposed he should be glad the child was no longer suffering. But what of the mother? She must have been desperate to do such a thing.

When he had tentatively conveyed his thoughts to Sergeant Harris he had been told in no uncertain terms that it was not his concern. 'Forget it,' the sergeant had told him. 'There's nothing you can do about it. Besides, your job is to catch thieves and burglars. Leave murder to the detectives,' he said.

The word had been spoken with a flicker of contempt. Ordinary coppers were still a bit suspicious of the newly formed detective force, who didn't wear uniform and seemed to think themselves a bit above the constable on the beat. Another cause of resentment was that they did not have to work their way up through the ranks, a circumstance which Sergeant Harris had spoken out against.

Jeremiah knew better than to let the sergeant know that he had ambitions to join the detectives himself one day. Since coming to London some years ago he had come to know the dark alleys and rat-ridden courts of the area he patrolled as well as he knew the fields and woods of his native Norfolk. And he had come to realise that there was more to policing than chasing thieves who had stolen a loaf of bread or an apple to stave off their hunger; more to it than wading in with his truncheon to break up a drunken fight outside a pub.

In the years working with his gamekeeper father on the squire's estate he had developed a keen power of observation. He now applied this to his police work and it had helped him to make several arrests. But he knew that, as a detective in plain clothes, he would be in a better position to keep an eye on a suspicious character. At present, when he walked into a tavern, the sight of his uniform tended to make the customers clam up.

Since meeting Ruby, Jeremiah had become motivated by more than ambition. A constable living in the station house was not allowed to marry. But, as a detective he would earn more money and would be able to provide for a wife and family far better than if he had remained a gamekeeper's assistant in his native village. He was a patient man. He'd achieve both his ambitions one day – become a detective and win Ruby's heart. Meantime he'd carry on doing the best job he could.

Chapter Nine

The opportunity to confide in Fanny never occurred. Since the arrival of Polly, Mrs Andrews had insisted that Ruby was not needed above stairs and she would be of more use in the kitchen.

The servants were run ragged with preparations for the party which was in two days' time. Ruby had just emptied the water jugs in the scullery and had re-filled them ready for Fanny to take upstairs when Mrs Andrews called her.

'These potatoes are no good – they're all green. I'll have to have a word with the greengrocer,' she said. 'He might get away with delivering rubbish to some houscholds but not this one.' She threw the offending vegetables into the bin. 'You'll have to run to the market for me.'

She thrust a piece of paper into Ruby's hand and a few coins. 'Just the potatoes today. And don't be too long, mind.'

It was a crisp cold day and Ruby wrapped her shawl round her shoulders and hurried out of the side gate. The market was only a few streets away and it didn't take long to fill her basket. The sounds and smells of the market tempted her to linger but she dare not risk the sharp edge of Mrs Andrews's tongue or, worse still, a whack with the wooden spoon, if she were gone too long. Reluctantly she turned away from the haberdashery stall and its piles of rainbow silks.

As she stepped back her basket caught someone's arm and she turned to apologise, blushing furiously as she realised who it was. Despite her resolve to put Jeremiah out of her mind, she had harboured a small hope that she would bump into him again. Now that she had, she didn't know what to say.

'I can't stop,' she stammered. 'I don't want to get into trouble with Mrs Andrews.'

She tried to pass him but he took hold of her arm and turned her to face him. 'Ruby, what's the matter?'

She looked up at him and her heart gave a little flutter. Would it be so wrong just to pass the time of day with him?

'I didn't mean to alarm you,' he said, a blush creeping up his neck as he spoke. 'I'm so pleased I bumped into you.'

'Why?' Her voice came out a bit sharper than she had intended and it was her turn to blush.

His blush deepened. 'I – I – wanted to get to know you better.'

Ruby was pleased but she knew there was no point in encouraging him. He wouldn't want to even speak to her once he found out about her condition.

'I must get back, Constable Locker,' she said, quickening her footsteps.

'I know you're in a hurry but please, let me walk with you.' His blue eyes twinkled. 'And didn't we agree that you were going to call me Jerry?'

'All right – Jerry,'

He laughed and kept pace with her as she hurried along and gradually she relaxed and found herself answering his questions about her life at Exton House. 'It's not bad, but I'm thinking of leaving, finding another job.'

'I thought the Prestons were good employers. Why would you leave?'

'I've never been out of London. I thought it might be nicer in the country.'

'London's not so bad. I like it here anyway. I grew up in the country.'

Ruby realised that was why he talked so strangely. His soft country accent was so different from the harsh London vowels. She felt she could listen to him all day but before she knew it they were at the corner of Warwick Square and she stopped. "I must go or I'll get into trouble.'

'I'd really like to see you again. When's your next day off?'

'I sometimes get an afternoon off as well as one Sunday a month usually but not while we have guests. Too much to do.'

'I'll look out for you when I'm passing then,' Jeremiah said.

She went in by the side gate, her heart racing. The more she saw of him, the more she liked him. After that first encounter in the market she had hoped that they would become more than friends. But now... If only they'd met months ago, before Oliver Preston had forced himself on her, she thought.

When she entered the kitchen she met a torrent of anger. 'Where have you been all this time?' Mrs Andrews shouted. 'How can I be expected to do my work when I'm surrounded by lazy good-for-nothing girls?'

Ruby endured the scolding. It was worth it. Just for a little while she'd been able to forget the nagging worry of what would happen to her when her pregnancy was discovered – as it surely would be before long. She made her escape as soon as she could and went in search of Fanny.

* * *

Jeremiah watched from the corner until Ruby had disappeared down the area steps into the basement of Exton House. He should have been investigating yet another burglary in the area and was supposed to be meeting up with his sergeant to compare notes. But he hadn't been able to pass up the opportunity of furthering his acquaintance with Ruby.

And now, after spending such a short time with her, he knew it wasn't just her looks that attracted him. She was bright and intelligent with a sense of fun. In their short walk from the market she had told him about being an orphan and having spent all her life either in the

Foundling Hospital or skivvying for the Prestons. But her hard life had not dampened her spirit. His heart had sunk when she'd told him she wanted to find a job in the country. Perhaps he should have impressed on her that country life could be just as hard as in the city.

He fingered the red ribbon which he still carried in his pocket. He'd been tempted to give it to her today but felt he didn't know her well enough yet. He didn't want to frighten her off. Next time they met he vowed to pluck up the courage.

As he passed the mews he heard raised voices and stopped to investigate. A young man was holding onto a horse's bridle with one hand while waving his riding crop in the coachman's face. Spittle flew from his lips as he shouted. 'This is a very valuable animal, Williams. I will not have him spooked by stupid children playing around in the yard when they should be at school or better still at work.'

Jeremiah watched as the coachman touched his forehead deferentially and said, 'Very sorry, sir. I'll see it doesn't happen again.'

His manner seemed to calm the young man. 'I'm sure you will, Williams,' he said. But his voice was cold as he added, 'You know the consequences if you don't keep your brats under control. Now, help me to mount if you please.'

Williams linked his hands to provide a step up for his employer and the young man swung his leg over the horse's back and settled himself in the saddle. As he urged the stallion forward he shouted over his shoulder, 'Don't let me catch sight of those boys again or you'll all be out on your ear.' He clattered out of the yard without seeming to notice Jeremiah's presence.

He had watched the scene in silence knowing it was more than his job was worth to intervene, although he knew he would have if that arrogant young buck had struck the servant with the riding crop. He seethed at the injustice of it, remembering similar scenes from his childhood back on the Thorleigh estate when his father had often been threatened with eviction from his cottage for some minor misdemeanour.

So that must be the son of the house, Oliver Preston, he thought. He and his parents had still been in Scotland when the house opposite, as well as several in the area, had been burgled. Many of the gentry went to the country during the shooting season and criminals took the opportunity of striking at those houses where there were few servants remaining and discipline was a bit lax. Jeremiah was surprised that Exton House had escaped. Perhaps they'd been due for a visit from the gang but the attack on the night watchman had deterred them. Waiting for the heat to die down, Jeremiah thought.

He was about to walk away when he noticed Alfie, the little boy he'd encountered before, emerging from his hiding place behind a pile of straw. He was followed by another, a little older. Their father bent down and opened his arms and the lads ran towards him to be enfolded in a warm embrace. 'Sorry, Dad. We didn't mean to get you into trouble,' the biggest one said.

'We was playing with Smoky and he ran away. It was him frightened the horse, Dad. It wasn't us,' said Alfie.

'It's all right, lads. It wasn't your fault. Mister Oliver's in a bad mood this morning,' the man said.

'He's always in a bad mood,' the younger child said.

'Hush, Alfie.' Williams stood up. 'Now, go indoors and keep out of the way.'

Alfie turned and spotted Jeremiah in the mews entrance. He clutched his father's leg. 'There's that policeman again, Dad,' he said, his eyes wide.

'Don't worry, son. Run along inside.' Williams shooed the boys towards the outside stairs leading to the apartments over the stables and crossed the yard towards Jeremiah.

'Something wrong, Constable?' he asked.

'No. I was just passing and heard the commotion.'

'I try to keep the boys out of the way when the master's son's around. He don't like children, you see.' His lips twisted wryly.

'I could tell,' Jeremiah said with a smile.

'No news on the burglaries then?'

'Afraid not. We're still pursuing our inquiries as we say. It's a pity the servants always come under suspicion.' Jeremiah decided to take the man into his confidence.

'We're pretty sure it's a gang from over Whitechapel way. They aren't working alone though. They must have someone on the inside letting them know which families are away. There's been another burglary just round the corner - they hadn't even left a caretaker to keep an eye on the place. The word soon gets round – servants' gossip, tradespeople.'

'The Prestons never leave the place unattended. They travelled by train last time and only took a few of servants with them. And I take care to keep my eyes and ears open while they're away.'

'Don't worry – we'll get them in the end and then it's off to Botany Bay with them.'

'Let's hope so.'

Jeremiah wasn't sure he should have confided in the coachman. He might have his suspicions that all was not well at Exton House but he was sure Williams wasn't involved. He seemed an honest, hard-working family man. But he had learned in his short time in the police force that you should never judge by appearances. He looked round the yard, inhaling the pungent scent of hay and horse manure. It reminded him of home.

'Do you like your work, Williams?' he asked.

'I've always loved horses. And we're lucky really, I suppose – warm comfortable quarters and good employers.'

Jeremiah must have looked sceptical and Williams gave a short laugh. 'Sir Charles and

Lady Anne I mean. And the daughters are charming girls. But young Mister Oliver – well…'

He didn't have to say any more. Jeremiah had seen for himself what an unpleasant person the young master was.

Chapter Ten

It was the day of the party and Ruby was too busy to worry about being caught by Oliver. Besides, with the number of guests staying in the house there were too many people about. She still tried to make sure she was never alone upstairs though.

At least he never ventured into the kitchen she thought as she scurried along the passageway and down the basement stairs. She opened the door on pandemonium. Polly was crying over a pool of milk spreading amid the shards of a broken jug, while Cook berated her, waving a wooden spoon threateningly in her face.

Ruby carried the jugs through to the scullery and emptied the dirty water into the sink. Leaving Kitty to rinse them out ready for the refilling, she went back into the kitchen and tried to comfort the other kitchen maid. 'I'm sure she didn't mean to drop it, Mrs Andrews,' she said, trying to placate her. 'We'll soon clear it up.' She bent and began to pick up the broken shards of pottery.

'Meanwhile what are we going to do for milk?' Cook asked.

'I'll run to the dairy for more,' Ruby offered.

'All right, but don't let Mrs Catchpole see you. She was really cross when I sent you out the other day.'

Ruby wrapped a shawl round her shoulders and picked up a big jug, glad to be out of the house once more – and not just to be free from worry about being accosted by the son of the house. She knew she should put the encounter with Jerry Locker out of her mind but she couldn't help hoping she'd bump into him again. She hurried to the corner of the square and waited for a horse and carriage to pass before crossing the road and making her way down a narrow lane.

The dairy was set back from the road and she could hear the soft lowing of the cows in their stall behind the shop. A sign showing the head of a brown cow swung over the doorway. Ruby loved visiting the dairy with its clean tiled walls depicting country scenes of grazing cattle beside a stream. It was these pictures that had made her think she'd like to move to the country. It must be wonderful to live in a place where you could breathe fresh air and walk beside clear flowing water.

As she heaved a big sigh and put her hand on the door latch, it opened and Jeremiah came out, almost knocking her over.

He stammered apologies and she smiled up at him. 'Not your fault, sir. No harm done.'

'I thought you were going to call me Jerry now we're friends,' he said. 'In fact, I'd like us to be more than friends.'

Her heart hammered and she felt the blush creeping up her neck as it always did when she encountered him. She shouldn't encourage him but it was hard not to respond to that smile, those twinkling blue eyes. 'We'll see,' she said, holding up the jug. 'But I can't discuss it now. I have to get the milk or Mrs Andrews will be after me.'

She took her jug to the counter and the dairyman filled it from the huge churn. Hurrying outside, she saw Jeremiah standing at the corner of the lane. When she came up to him he walked alongside her.

'Just making sure you get home safely,' he said.

As she started down the area steps he called her back. Blushing and fumbling in his breast pocket, he drew out the length of scarlet ribbon. 'Just so you don't forget me,' he said.

She took the ribbon and smoothed it between her fingers. Tucking it into her apron pocket, she said softly, 'I won't forget.'

Mrs Andrews greeted her with relief and this time didn't comment on how long she'd been gone. The mess had now been cleared up, the kitchen maids were calmly going about their work and the housekeeper didn't seem to have noticed her absence.

Soon Ruby was back in the fray with the other servants, all anxious to get the preparations for the party finished. There was no time to dwell on her encounter with the handsome police constable, although from time to time she fingered the length of ribbon in her apron pocket.

The party went well and there were no further mishaps. Ruby, on one of her frequent trips back to the kitchen reported that the guests all seemed to be enjoying themselves, exclaiming over the lavish food that Cook and her kitchen maids had slaved over, as well as the elaborate decorations in the dining and ball rooms.

At last, the musicians packed up and went home and the family and guests went to their rooms. The dishes were washed and put away, fires banked down and the lamps extinguished. Exhausted, the servants could finally relax round the big scrubbed table. But, too tired to do justice to the supper of party leftovers, they soon retired to their quarters, thankful that the wedding would be taking place in Yorkshire in the spring – and not in London.

Despite her exhaustion, Ruby still found the strength to push the chest in front of her bedroom door before falling into bed. She just hoped it would be enough to deter Oliver if he decided to come to her room to try and assault her again. During the evening she had kept a wary eye on him and. although he had appeared to be lavishing all his attention on his bride to be, she had caught him glaring at her from time to time. He had been drinking steadily and she hoped he would be too drunk to creep up the attic stairs after everyone had retired. But she wasn't taking any chances.

Snuggled up in bed she allowed herself to relive the encounter with Jeremiah Locker. 'Jerry,' she murmured, savouring the name. Each time she saw him she fell more deeply in love and she lived for the moment she would see him again. But as she drifted off to sleep she thought sadly that there could be no future in a relationship with him. She had always vowed that if she ever married she would keep no secrets from her husband and she had the feeling that a man of the law like Constable Locker would not accept a wife who'd borne an illegitimate child and given it away.

With a little sob, she closed her eyes. At least she wouldn't be bothered by Oliver – the heavy chest in front of the door would see to that.

The following morning Ruby was down on her knees scrubbing the flagstones in the corridor leading to the tradesman's entrance in the basement area. She gasped and sat back on her heels as a sharp pain circled her body. She had been suffering from backache for several days but had put it down to the extra work due to the party preparations. But this was something completely different. The pain subsided for a moment then gripped her again. As she realised what was happening she felt a mixture of guilt and relief.

If she could just get through the day she could climb up to her attic and let nature take its course. If only the girls she shared her attic room with slept as soundly as they usually did. .

She took a few deep breaths and the pain eased. Trying to ignore the nagging worry at the back of her mind, she finished cleaning the floor and went back to the scullery to tip the dirty water away.

Before she could take a breath it was on to the next job and, trying to ignore the increasing frequency of the pains, she struggled to do her work and not arouse suspicion in her fellow servants.

It was almost midnight by the time her work was done. Fanny had gone home and Mrs Andrews was dozing in her chair by the range. Mr Phelps, the butler, and Hetty Catchpole had retired to his pantry for a nightcap and Silas, the valet, was in the laundry room getting the master's clothes ready for the morning. Gladys was upstairs helping the mistress to get ready for bed and the other servants had all retired for the night.

As Ruby was about to go up to her own bed, the cook stirred and looked round. 'Everyone abed?' she asked.

Ruby nodded. 'I'm just off myself. Goodnight, Mrs Andrews.'

'Just a minute, Ruby. Be a good girl and fetch some coal up from the cellar would you? That lazy boy's let it get too low and we can't have the range going out. It's a devil to get

114

going in the morning. When you've done that be sure to turn the gas lamp out before you go up.'

With an inward groan Ruby picked up the coal scuttle and opened the cellar door. There was no gas lighting down here and she took a candle to light her way.

By the time the coal scuttle was half full the pains were coming faster. One more shovelful and that would have to do. She had to get upstairs to her room – now. As she tried to lift the bucket another pain tore through her and, at the same time, she felt a gush of wetness between her legs. She dropped the shovel and clutched her stomach, groaning.

'Help – somebody help me, please,' she moaned, staggering towards the cellar steps. In her haste she tripped against the bottom step and fell to the ground. The pains increased in intensity and Ruby prayed aloud. She had never dreamed such pain existed.

Finally it was over and she tried to stand. She retrieved the candle from the ledge where she'd left it and gasped at the sight the light revealed. How would she explain this if anyone saw the mess? She took off her apron and tried to wipe away the stains from the steps. She was so intent on her task that at first the blaze of light didn't register. The voice did though and she shrank back into the darkness.

'Who's down there? Come out or I'll call the constable.' The lamp swung to and fro sending shadows dancing on the wall as Hetty Catchpole started down the stairs. 'Oh, it's you,

Ruby. What are you doing down here at this time of night?'

Ruby took a deep shuddering breath and managed to say, 'I came down for some coal and slipped on the stairs. I'm all right, Mrs Catchpole.'

'Are you sure?' The housekeeper held the lamp higher. 'You're hurt. There's blood...' Her voice trailed away. 'Oh, Ruby, you wicked girl. How could you?'

Ruby began to cry. 'It wasn't my fault. He made me. I didn't want to.'

Mrs Catchpole made a disgusted sound. 'That's what they all say.' She came down the stairs and set the lamp on a shelf. 'Well, what are we going to do with you?'

Ruby's tears fell faster. 'Please, don't send me to the workhouse – please.'

Mrs Catchpole pursed her lips. 'Stay here a moment – I'll fetch some water.'

Ruby gulped back her sobs, wondering what would happen to her now. She supposed she should have been thankful that this had happened. If only she had been able to get back to her room without being caught. She could only pray that Mrs Catchpole would not inform her employers. It would mean the workhouse for sure.

She tried to stand up but her legs felt weak and she sank back on to the cellar steps.

The housekeeper returned a few minutes later carrying a bowl of warm water and a cloth. 'Here, clean yourself up. Hurry up.'

'Thank you, Mrs Catchpole,' Ruby whispered.

'Now, give that filthy apron to me. I'll dispose of it. We don't want the rest of the household finding out what's happened, do we?'

Ruby shook her head and started to wash the blood stains from her legs.

Mrs Catchpole watched her for a moment, then gave a big sigh. 'You girls will keep getting yourselves into trouble. Well, let this be a lesson to you. I might not be here to help next time. Now, be sure to clean up thoroughly before you go to bed. There must be no sign of what happened here tonight.' She started up the stairs. 'Best you stay in bed tomorrow. I'll tell everyone you've got a touch of the flu. You've been looking a bit poorly lately so there won't be any suspicions.'

'Thank you, Mrs Catchpole,' Ruby whispered.

'You can thank me by being a good girl from now on. Just do your work and no more misbehaving.'

Ruby wanted to protest that she wasn't the one who'd misbehaved. But what was the use? The girl was always in the wrong. Even the housekeeper, who was being so kind to her, thought it was her own fault she'd got into trouble as they called it.

It wasn't until she was back in her room that it occurred to her to wonder what Mrs Catchpole had been doing down in the cellar after everyone had gone to bed. Perhaps she had

117

heard a noise and thought it was burglars. Still, Ruby thought, as she tried to get to sleep, perhaps it was a good thing she had turned up when she did. But why had she been so kind to her?

* * *

Hetty Catchpole wasn't being kind at all. Her devious mind was wondering how she could turn the situation to her advantage. Finding the girl in the cellar had given her a dreadful fright. She knew that Ruby was more intelligent than the average housemaid and when she heard about the latest burglary she might have started to put two and two together. It had been such a relief to realise that the girl was suffering a miscarriage and that burglars were the last thing on her mind.

Hetty made it her business to be aware of everything that went on in the household from the master himself down to the lowliest scullery maid. She had seen the lustful looks that Mister Oliver had directed at Ruby and she knew about his visit to the maids' attic just before he'd gone away last time. For weeks she had watched Ruby like a hawk, waiting for the telltale signs that the girl was pregnant. She knew she could make some money out of it while at the same time pretending to help as she had with previous maids. It was a shame the girl had lost the baby – she'd had plans for it. But still, catching Ruby tonight had given her a hold over the girl.

It wasn't just 'helping' girls who had got into trouble that supplemented Hetty Catchpole's income. She and her nephew Silas also had their share from the burglaries. But now that she'd found Ruby down in the basement when she should have been in bed she couldn't help wondering if the girl had seen something she shouldn't. They would have to be extra careful from now on.

Before going to her own bed, she wrapped the evidence of the miscarriage in newspaper and, picking up the lamp, went back down to the cellar. She pushed the parcel well to the back of the pile of coal, making sure it was well out of sight. She smiled. It was unlikely to be discovered any time soon and, if it was, Hetty had her story ready. As for the soiled apron, she would hang on to that. It was something to hold over Ruby if it ever became necessary.

Chapter Eleven

Ruby had recovered from the miscarriage and it now seemed like a bad dream. She was still wary of the housekeeper however and kept out of her way as much as possible. She was still puzzled as to why Mrs Catchpole had been so kind to her, although that softening of her attitude hadn't lasted long. But as time went by, she tried to put it our of her mind, only thankful that it was all over and that no one except the housekeeper had any idea of what had happened .

At least she had no fear of it happening again – for the moment at least. To her relief Oliver had left Exton House to spend Christmas with his fiancée and her parents at Brampton Hall.

The day after he left, Ruby woke feeling more light-hearted than she had for ages. She even wondered optimistically if she might be sent out on an errand. Although she had resolved to put Jeremiah firmly out of her head, she couldn't help wishing she could see him once more.

It was unlikely she'd be allowed to leave the house today though. The servants were busy with preparations for Christmas and none of the servants had a minute to themselves. The big kitchen was full of steam and the scent of the huge joints of beef and pork which were roasting in the oven and Mrs Andrews was busy dressing the goose, which was to be the centrepiece of the Christmas dinner.

Ruby had got her appetite back at last and the smells were tantalising. As she and Kitty washed the best serving dishes in the scullery she felt almost faint with hunger.

'It'll be just bread and cheese for us today,' Kitty said.

'Well, it's not Christmas yet,' Ruby replied.

'I can't wait,' said Kitty. 'We always has a special dinner on Christmas day and then there's the presents…'

When they sat down for their bread and cheese, Mr Phelps cleared his throat, causing them all to look up expectantly. 'I'm sorry to inform you that there has been another burglary over the way at Lord Jameson's place.'

His words caused a flurry of anxiety and Kitty, the more nervous of the kitchen maids, burst into hysterical tears, crying, 'We'll all be murdered in our beds.'

Mrs Andrews rounded on her, giving her a hefty slap round the face. 'Stop your nonsense girl. No one's going to break in here while Mr Phelps and Silas and Archie are around.' She gave a sarcastic laugh. 'We can't count Jimmy,' she said.

The boot boy, despite his earlier show of bravado, had been looking just as scared as the maids when Kitty had started her wailing.

Mr Phelps thumped the table and called them to order. 'There is no cause for alarm. Sir

Charles is having new locks installed on all the doors.'

Mrs Andrews gave another sarcastic laugh but the butler quelled her with a look.

'The police are making regular patrols and I'm sure they'll catch the gang before long,' he said.

'They haven't made a very good job of it so far, have they?' said Mrs Andrews.

Ruby almost spoke up for the police, especially Jerry. But she hastily swallowed the exclamation that rose to her lips. It wouldn't do for anyone to realise how friendly she had become with the policeman.

* * *

The long day came to a close but before she could go up to bed, Ruby's last job was to bank up the fire so that it did not go out overnight. She knelt in front of the range and reached for the coal scuttle, tutting in annoyance when she saw it was empty. Jimmy should have filled it before going to bed.

She stood up and took a few reluctant steps towards the cellar, remembering the last time she'd been down there. Aside from the bad memories, she had always hated going along the dark passage past the storerooms to reach the cellar. She took a candle from the shelf just inside the door to light her way and opened the cellar door.

When she'd filled the coal scuttle she dragged herself up the stairs, groaning under the weight. As she turned to close the door, a draught almost blew out the candle but the flame steadied and she made her way down the passage towards the kitchen. The flame flickered again and she noticed the door to one of the storerooms was ajar.

Most of the everyday crockery and utensils were kept in the kitchen on shelves or hung from hooks in the ceiling. But the things that were only used occasionally were kept here, along with several items of unused furniture and fittings from the main house. Putting down the heavy coal scuttle, Ruby pushed the door open and held up the candle. A small window high up on the wall which gave on to the mews was open. Surely Mr Phelps should have gone round and made sure all was secure before going to bed?

She went across to close the window, starting as a sharp voice behind her said, 'Oh, it's you, Ruby. What are you doing down here at this time of night?' Mrs Catchpole held her lamp up to Ruby's face and looked at her suspiciously.

'I had to get coal for the range and I saw the window open. I thought I ought to close it – especially since there's been all this talk of burglars.'

'I'll see to it,' the housekeeper said. 'You get on up to bed.' She watched Ruby struggling to pick up the heavy bucket of coal, saying,

'Silas or Jimmy should have done that. I'll speak to them about it in the morning. You shouldn't have to struggle with that heavy scuttle.'

Ruby didn't know what to say. It wasn't like the housekeeper to sound sympathetic. She went into the kitchen and kneeled to make up the fire. When she was sure she had caught it in time, she damped it down with coal dust and closed the damper. That should keep it going till morning, she thought, sitting back on her heels and wiping her hands on her coarse apron. She fingered the outline of the precious ribbon through the material and was about to take it out of her pocket when she heard Mrs Catchpole coming along the passage. What had she been doing all this time?

'I thought I told you to go to bed,' the housekeeper snapped. 'Run along at once.'

Ruby hastened up the back stairs to her room, expecting to find the other maids already fast asleep. But they were still awake.

Kitty jumped when Ruby opened the door. 'Oh, it's you. Where have you been? I daren't go to sleep till you came up.'

'You're not really nervous are you?' Ruby asked.

Kitty nodded, her eyes large in her white face.

'Come on then, let's drag the chest across. No one can get in while that's in front of the door.'

As they had every night since they'd first heard of the break-ins, the girls pushed the chest which contained their meagre belongings across the room. As far as Ruby was concerned there was no need now that Oliver was no longer here to torment her. But it put Kitty's mind at rest. It didn't seem to occur to the kitchen maids that the servants' attics wouldn't offer very rich pickings. Any potential burglar would have no reason to come up here. They'd be concentrating on the valuables in the downstairs rooms.

* * *

Jeremiah had not seen Ruby for some time and he wished he could find an excuse to walk past Exton House. But Sergeant Harris had put him on a different beat and he dared not deviate from it. His only consolation was that he still had to walk through the market where he'd bumped into her before and there was always the chance that she'd be sent on another errand. A glimpse of her would brighten up his day.

Perhaps he had been mistaken in thinking that she returned his interest. But she had accepted the gift of the red ribbon with a gracious smile and he dared to hope that meant she felt something for him.

His thoughts of Ruby did not distract him from his duties and he was alert for any criminal activity as he walked along the riverside where barges were unloading their goods at the wharves.

Thieves and pickpockets abounded in this area, mingling with the crowds and easily managing to escape in the confusion of watermen, dockers and bargees. Sometimes, the sight of a patrolling policeman was sufficient to deter them but many of them were defiantly bold.

He turned away into a narrow street of terraced houses and remembered that he had been here before in the course of his inquiries into the drowned child. The house on the end of the row was the home of a child minder and they had questioned her closely, but to no avail. They saw no obvious signs of neglect or ill-treatment of the children in her care and Jeremiah had to concede that, despite their suspicions, nothing could be done without evidence.

Frustrated, Jeremiah strode out briskly, leaving the street behind. It was a bright sunny day but bitterly cold with a chill wind off the river and he was anxious to get back to the station for his dinner. It had been a long day and his feet hurt after covering many miles in the course of his shift.

As he turned the corner he caught sight of a familiar figure and recognised Silas James, one of the footmen at Exton House. What was he doing here, so far from Warwick Square?

Jeremiah hurried after him thinking he might ask for news of Ruby. He remembered her telling him that she might change her job and, as it was some time since he'd last seen her, he wanted to make sure she was still working for the Prestons.

He had almost caught up with Silas when another man came out of a house at the end of the row and the two men stopped to exchange greetings. They seemed to be arguing and Jeremiah stopped and concealed himself in a nearby doorway. He wasn't sure what had aroused his suspicions but there was something furtive about the way they had glanced round before continuing their conversation. Jeremiah wished he could hear what they were saying.

When he and Sergeant Harris had questioned the servants at Exton House he had not taken to Silas James at all. Although the footman had answered their questions readily enough and seemed just as shocked as everyone else by the attack on the watchman there had been something almost insolent in his manner. His smile was sly as he said, 'I hope you catch the blackguards, sir.'

Now, as the men parted, Jeremiah was determined to speak to Silas. Not wishing to reveal that he had seen him and his companion, he dodged into the alley that ran behind the houses. He calculated that it would come out in the next street and if he hurried he would meet Silas coming the other way. He would act as if it were a chance meeting.

The footman spotted him straight away and Jeremiah was gratified to see the momentary consternation on the other man's face. It was quickly replaced by an obsequious smile as Jeremiah asked what he was doing so far from home.

'Not so far, Constable.' He gestured towards the row of houses. 'This is my home, leastways it was until I went into service. It's my day off and I've been visiting my old ma.'

It was a plausible enough explanation and had a ring of truth. But that furtive exchange with the shifty-looking man had set Jeremiah thinking. It could have just been a chance meeting between two old acquaintances but, although he had no proof of any wrongdoing, he had a feeling in his gut that Silas James was up to no good.

He forced a smile and said, 'Your mother's lucky to have such a dutiful son.'

'You're telling me,' the other man replied. 'It's a long walk down here just to make sure the old girl's all right and to slip her a few coppers for a bottle of gin.'

Jeremiah gave a sympathetic smile, then changed the subject as the man seemed about to walk away. 'By the way, you must have heard that the night watchman had recovered?'

Silas nodded. 'It could have been a bad business,' he muttered.

'Well, at least whoever was responsible has escaped a murder charge.'

Silas gave a sly grin. 'That's if you coppers ever catch whoever did it.'

'Oh, we'll catch them all right – eventually - and then it will be off to Botany Bay for them,' Jeremiah said.

Silas just smirked and Jeremiah felt anger burning in his chest. He forced a smile and changed the subject. 'It's a pleasant day. I hope you enjoy the rest of your time off.'

'Well, I had planned to do something better than traipsing down here to see Ma,' he said. 'I had my eye on that little Fanny Williams – leastways I did. Thought I was in with a chance till Sir Charles's valet came back. Seems she and Archie Bass have an understanding.' He gave a coarse laugh. 'Still, she's not the only maid at Exton House.'

His smile was more of a leer and Jeremiah's thoughts flew to Ruby. He kept his voice neutral and said, 'Anyone in particular? I seem to remember a housemaid called Ruby.'

'No chance. Mrs Catchpole wouldn't let her go today; she's got tomorrow afternoon off. Pity we couldn't have the same day.'

Jeremiah made his excuses and hurried away before he could reveal his real feelings. He felt sorry for the young girls who had to work alongside a man like Silas James. But as he strode away his heart was light and there was a spring in his step, his aching feet forgotten. Ruby was not only still employed at Exton House, she would be free the next day. He would try to swap shifts with one of his mates so that he could be sure of seeing her.

Back at the police station he sought out Inspector Higgins at his desk and told him about the meeting with Silas James and his suspicions that he might have been involved in the burglaries.

'We know the gang comes from around there,' he said. 'I think James may be using visits to his mother as an excuse to be in the area and meet up with his cronies,' he said. 'He didn't sound as if he has much affection for her anyway. But he grew up around there and he must be acquainted with our suspects.'

Sergeant Harris tapped his pencil on the desk and looked thoughtful. 'You may be right, Constable. But we have no proof and until then we can do nothing. Besides, the case had been handed over to the detective branch. It's out of our hands now.'

Jeremiah was disappointed, although he had guessed what the sergeant's reaction would be. If only he could be transferred to the detectives. But it was unlikely they'd accept the application of a lowly constable. He would have to prove himself first.

He took out his notebook and read what he had written there. At least if he had to give evidence at any future trial he would have a record of his observations.

Thinking of trials reminded him that he had to attend the Old Bailey the following week to give evidence in a case involving theft from a coal merchant. An employee had been delivering short measures to the merchant's customers, selling the surplus on to an accomplice. The householder had complained and Jeremiah had watched for some weeks until he caught the man in the act.

Another case solved, he thought with satisfaction. If only they were all like that. But policing wasn't that easy. So many criminals went unpunished. His throat tightened as he recalled that they had never caught the murderer of the baby found in the river and, since then there had been others.

Chapter Twelve

Ruby liked to go out on her rare afternoons off. Although she had no family or friends to visit and seldom had more than a few coppers to spend she still liked to get away from Exton House as often as possible. Her experience in the cellar on that dreadful night had left her nervous and apprehensive of any encounter with the housekeeper. She dreaded Mrs Catchpole bringing it up and berating her for her so-called wicked behaviour. Besides, if she stayed in during her free time, someone would find some work for her to do.

It had been all right during the better weather when she could wander round the market enjoying the colourful sights and sounds of the street traders. But the last couple of weeks had been cold and damp with fog coming up from the river and she had resigned herself to staying in her room today.

She was sure that her free time would be stopped as they were so busy – it was the day before Christmas Eve and there was still so much to do. Mrs Catchpole was in a worse mood than usual and although Ruby had been kept busy in the kitchens all morning she knew that the housekeeper would find something for her to do upstairs if she caught sight of her. Despite having a new housemaid, there always seemed to be too much for her and Fanny to do.

Ruby had spent the whole morning washing the breakfast dishes and then peeling potatoes and carrots while Kitty and Annie scrubbed pans in the scullery and she was looking forward to a rest. Although she had made a complete recovery from her miscarriage, she still tired easily and by the time she had finished her dinner she was ready to go upstairs and lie down. What else was there to do in this dreadful weather? Besides, she had plenty of mending to keep her occupied.

As she got her needles and thread from the chest, a shaft of pale sunlight lit a corner of the room. The fog had cleared at last. She went over to the dormer window, looking across the rooftops to the trees in the square. Their branches were bare now, outlined against the cold blue sky. The air was chill but the sun had chased away the fog. Perhaps she would go out today after all. There was always the chance that she would bump into Jerry again. What harm in having a friendly chat, she thought, although she would have to be careful not to betray her true feelings.

Dressing quickly, she brushed her hair and began to pin it up in its usual bun. Then she smiled to herself. It was her afternoon off after all. She pulled out the hairpins and took the red ribbon that Jeremiah had given her from under her pillow. She tied her abundant curls back with it and, pulling her shawl over her head to hide the ribbon, she hurried down the back stairs.

As she went to slip out of the back door, she heard Mrs Catchpole mentioning her name. 'Where's Ruby? There's all the silver still to polish you know.'

Oh no, if the housekeeper saw her she would never get away. She paused in the shadows and breathed a sigh of relief at Mrs Andrews's reply.

'Have you forgotten it's her afternoon off? The girl works hard enough, doesn't she?'

Hetty's reply was an inelegant snort. 'She's just doing the job she's paid for,' she said. 'These girls get far too much free time. When I was a girl we were lucky to get one day off every quarter – what's the world coming to?'

Ruby didn't wait to hear the cook's reply. She crept out and across the yard, looking back once to make sure she hadn't been spotted.

She wished she and Fanny could have time off together. She hardly had a chance to talk to her friend since the visitors had gone home and she wasn't needed upstairs so much. It would have been nice to have someone to go out with. But her friend spent all her free time with Archie these days. On their last afternoon off the couple had taken Fanny's little brothers to the park.

The next day she'd come in bubbling over with excitement. 'We had such a lovely time yesterday,' she said, laughing. 'There was a hurdy-gurdy man with a little monkey. You should have seen Alfie and Billy's faces.'

Remembering how enthusiastic Fanny had been, Ruby thought she might go to the park too. She had no money to spend in the market and besides, much as she longed to see Jerry again, she had told herself it would do no good to encourage him.

When she was out of sight of the house, she uncovered her hair, wrapping her shawl round her shoulders. It was the first time she'd dared to wear the ribbon for fear of comments from the other servants, but today she didn't care who saw.

It was such a lovely feeling, having someone who cared about her. But, much as she liked Jerry's company she knew there was no future in it. She had recovered physically from the miscarriage but the shame never left her. Jerry would never forgive her if he discovered what had happened to her. And even if he did, where was the sense in falling in love when she knew that it was only a matter of time before Oliver came home and forced himself on her again? She wouldn't be so lucky this time and when the inevitable happened Mrs Catchpole would pounce. Since finding Ruby in the cellar that night she had watched her intently for signs that Ruby had fallen again. And then it would be dismissal and the workhouse for sure.

The wind was cold and she pulled her shawl more closely around her. It was a long walk to the park and by the time she reached the gates her steps had slowed and she was feeling very tired. Perhaps she should have stayed at home and rested. But she was enjoying the unaccustomed feel of the sun on her face despite the cold wind. And the sight of people going about their everyday business cheered her up a little.

She strolled along the paths until she found an empty bench, sheltered by a group of evergreen shrubs. She sat down and closed her eyes, turning her face up to the sun. Out of the wind there was a little warmth in it, although it was well into winter. She was almost drifting off to sleep when she heard voices and she sat up and looked around. Two nannies in their smart uniforms were pushing perambulators along the path towards her. One of them leaned down towards the sleeping child and adjusted the blanket, smiling. The other one said something and they both laughed. They looked so contented and carefree and obviously loved the babies in their care.

Once Ruby had dreamed of having a child of her own to care for. Now she knew it would never happen. As Mrs Catchpole had said, having the miscarriage had probably been all for the best. But she still felt a pang of grief for the loss of her child, even if the poor little thing probably would have ended up in the Foundling Hospital just as she had. She leapt up with a small sob and hurried down the path away from them. By the time she reached the park gates the tears were falling in earnest. She couldn't go back to Exton House in this state. She stopped by the drinking fountain and, wetting the corner of her shawl, she wiped her face.

As she bent to take a drink of water from the fountain, she froze as a voice addressed her, 'Everything all right, Ruby?'

She whirled round, her face growing hot. 'Oh, it's you,' she said, gazing up into Jerry's concerned face.

'Ruby, you're crying. Has someone hurt you?' he asked.

'I'm not crying,' she protested. 'I had something in my eye.'

She could tell he didn't really believe her but he didn't comment. Instead he smiled and said, 'I'm glad I bumped into you.' He crooked his arm, inviting her to take it and said, 'Would you do me the honour of taking a little walk.'

She couldn't help smiling and she bobbed a mock curtsey. 'Thank you, kind sir.' She took his arm and they began to stroll along the paths between the flower beds, now sad stretches of bare earth waiting for the spring daffodils to appear. But Ruby was unconscious of her surroundings. She loved feeling the warmth of her hand tucked into his arm, the feel of the rough serge of his uniform coat against her skin. She savoured the moment, dreaming that one day they would always be together like this. It didn't hurt to dream.

'I see you're wearing the ribbon I gave you,' said Jeremiah.

'I have to pin my hair up when I'm working but I can please myself on my day off,' she said, blushing.

'And that's not any old ribbon, is it?' he said with a teasing smile.

'I don't have another,' she retorted and he laughed.

They walked in silence for a few moments until she said, 'Shouldn't you be working – catching burglars or something?'

'Not at the moment. I finished my shift at noon today.'

'Have you caught anyone yet?'

Jeremiah shook his head. 'We've a pretty good idea who's behind all the break-ins but we need proof. We think there's an inside man in one of the houses, a servant probably, who gives information about which owners are away, which houses offer the richest pickings. Servants talk to each other don't they?'

'Yes, there's always gossip below stairs. But I hope you don't suspect anyone in our household.'

'It could be anybody in any of those big houses.' He smiled down at her and shook his head. 'Let's not talk about my work. Anyway, what about you? Shouldn't you be scrubbing floors or whatever it is you do?'

'It's my afternoon off.'

'So what are you doing all alone in the park – you should be out with your friends, having fun.'

'The maids aren't allowed to take time off together and I don't have any other friends. Besides, I don't mind being alone.'

'Why were you crying? And don't tell me you had something in your eye.' Jeremiah stopped walking and pulled her round to face him. 'Tell me, Ruby, who's upset you?'

He looked angry and, although it warmed her heart to think that he cared enough to get upset on her behalf, she shook her head. She couldn't tell him – and she wouldn't lie. But she had to say something. 'No one really. It's just that I hate working at Exton House and I wasn't looking forward to going back. I told you I wanted to find another job, didn't I?'

'Well, why don't you?' Jeremiah asked.

'What's the point? I don't know anything but being in service. It just suddenly struck me that wherever I go my life won't really change.' It wasn't the truth but he seemed to accept it.

He took her arm again and they resumed their walk. Dusk was starting to fall and the park gates would be closing soon. It was time she was getting back. But she didn't want the afternoon to end.

Jeremiah must have felt the same for, as she went to pull away from him, he pulled her closer. 'I wish you didn't have to go,' he muttered.

She felt his breath, warm against her cheek. Then his hands were stroking her hair and he was kissing her, his lips soft yet firm against hers. Her arms went round him and she responded ardently. Her eyes were closed and she wished they could stay like this forever.

Footsteps on the path made them spring apart and Ruby turned away, patting her hair into place and straightening her shawl.

'Sorry, constable. I have to lock the gates.' It was the park keeper.

'We're just leaving anyway,' Jeremiah said calmly, taking Ruby's arm and leading her outside.

She was a little embarrassed. She had never dreamed she would behave like that in public and she just prayed the park keeper hadn't seen them. Still, it was a good thing he'd come along when he did, she thought. Things were beginning to get out of hand.

When they got to the corner of the avenue, Jeremiah burst into laughter. 'Oh, dear. That was no way for a respectable police officer to carry on, was it?' He stopped laughing and looked at Ruby. 'I'm sorry, my sweet. I didn't embarrass you, did I?' He took her hands and looked into her eyes, his voice serious now. 'I couldn't resist you, my dearest Ruby. I've been thinking about you since the day we first met. Please tell me you feel the same way about me.'

Ruby's heart was beating faster and she longed to say 'yes'. She loved him – loved his sudden bursts of laughter, his dedication to his work, most of all the way he made her feel so special. But she wasn't special and if he knew, he would change towards her. She couldn't bear the thought of his loving looks turning to disgust and hatred. The only way to prevent that was to never see him again.

But even as the thoughts rushed through her head she was conscious of his gaze as he waited for a reply. She felt the blood rush to her face and she nodded dumbly.

He smiled and said, 'Don't be shy, Ruby. Say it – say you love me.'

'I do – I love you,' she whispered, tears glistening on her lashes.

In a moment she was in his arms again as, careless of any passers-by, he kissed her again and again. And she returned the kisses in full measure. All the while the words pounded in her head. 'It's the last time. Savour these moments while you can.'

At last he released her and in silence they walked towards Warwick Square. Ruby didn't mind the silence; she was savouring those kisses, the feel of his lips on hers. She started when he said, 'I wasn't sure how you felt until I saw you wearing the ribbon I gave you.'

'It's beautiful – red's my favourite colour.'

'It matches your name,' he said, taking her hand. 'One day I'll buy you a ring – a ruby for my Ruby,' he said.

She didn't know what to say. It was never going to happen. For a moment she allowed herself to dream. He need never know what had happened with Oliver and if he found out, he'd understand – wouldn't he? 'I'd like that, Jerry,' she whispered, unwilling to shatter the dream and spoil these precious moments together.

They reached the corner of Warwick Square and he took her hand. 'I'd better leave you here. Don't want you to get into trouble.'

She hoped he would kiss her again but he just gave her hand a squeeze. 'I'll look out for you. Try to let me know when you next have an afternoon off.'

'I'll will,' she said. But even as she promised she knew she wouldn't. She knew she must not see him again despite their declaration of love.

She turned the corner, hoping the gate would be open. She could slip through the side door and up the back stairs without seeing anyone. She couldn't face going down the area steps and through the kitchen. They would all be there, wanting to know how she'd spent her time off. But her time with Jerry was too precious to share with anyone.

* * *

Jeremiah stood on the corner until Ruby was out of sight before turning his steps towards his lodgings. He walked briskly, whistling under his breath, blessing the chance that had led to him meeting Silas. He would never have known Ruby was not working today otherwise.

The thought of Silas James made him frown. He was sure the man had been up to no good but he couldn't put his finger on what had made him suspicious. Was it just that he didn't like the man, resented his suggestive remarks about Ruby? When he had voiced his suspicions to Inspector Higgins his boss had been sceptical. He knew that, unless he could find some real evidence, he would not be listened to.

There had been no more burglaries since the night watchman had been injured and Jeremiah thought that perhaps the gang were lying low till the heat died down. But then last night another house had been broken into while the owners were at the theatre. The servants claimed to have heard nothing, the butler protesting that he had let them go to bed early. He had waited up himself until his employers returned home and had then gone to bed himself, after locking the house securely. He had noticed nothing untoward and it wasn't until the following evening, when the lady of the house was dressing for dinner that she had discovered the loss of her diamond necklace. Further investigation revealed that most of her jewellery had been stolen as well as several items of silver from the dining room.

Jeremiah and his fellow constables had been despatched to visit all the known fences to try to recover the stolen goods but nothing had turned up. He guessed that the crooks had hidden the stuff somewhere, waiting until it was safe to get rid of it. Now, several days later, he had done another round of the places where they were likely to try and sell the stuff. But so far he'd had no luck.

When his shift had finished he had set out for Warwick Square, hoping to catch Ruby as she left the house. There had been no sign of her and, after hanging about for a while, he had turned away in disappointment. Wondering where she could have gone, he recalled her talking about the country. The nearest thing to country in this area was the large park nearby with its grass and trees and the lake in the centre. He had a feeling Ruby might have gone there and besides, even if he didn't catch up with her, it would be good to stroll in the fresh air. It was nothing like walking through the woods of home, of course, but as he kicked at the fallen leaves on the path, their scent took him back to his childhood and he felt a sudden burst of longing for his native county.

He had just decided that he was not going to be lucky today when he turned round and spotted Ruby by the drinking fountain. His heart lurched when he saw she was crying and he had rushed towards her.

He didn't believe her feeble excuse that she'd been upset because she hated her job. Unlike him, very few people actually enjoyed their work. It was a necessity for all but the very rich and most people just accepted it. There must be a reason for her tears and he was determined to find out what it was. And if he discovered that she was being bullied or ill-treated by anyone in the Preston household, be it master or servant, he would...

He clenched his fists and gritted his teeth. What could he do? Any interference on his part would surely result in more trouble for Ruby.

He resolved that he would get her away from there as soon as possible. They loved each other and, although he didn't earn very much as a constable, Inspector Higgins had hinted that he was in line for promotion. As a sergeant he'd be able to afford to get married. Once he'd found somewhere for them to live, he would propose to her.

* * *

Ruby lay on her bed crying. All the joy she had felt on her meeting with Jerry had turned to despair. For a few moments, the wonder of his kisses and the knowledge that he loved her had lifted her to unimaginable heights. She had dared to dream that such love would overcome all obstacles. But now she faced the fact that it most likely would never be.

She buried her face in the pillow, trying to stifle a further outburst of sobs. Should she have told him about Oliver? Would he be angry on her behalf? Or would he recoil from her? A man like Jeremiah, honest and upright, would surely want an innocent maid for a wife. Not one besmirched and spoiled by another man – even if it wasn't her fault.

She shuddered at the memory and a wave of hatred for Oliver Preston swelled in her breast. She pounded her fist into the pillow, wishing it was his face. Then she dried her tears and swore that he'd never get the chance to do that to her again.

The door opening brought her to her senses and she stood up as Kitty said, 'Oh, you're back. That's good. Mrs Catchpole says you're wanted downstairs.'

'I'll just be a minute,' she said. She brushed her hair and pinned it up, tucking the precious red ribbon into her apron pocket. Then she washed her face, hoping no one would notice the trace of tears. As she followed Kitty downstairs, she thought, so much for my afternoon off. There was always work to take her mind off her troubles.

'Did you have a good time?' Kitty asked.

'Yes, I went for a walk in the park,' Ruby replied, briefly raising her hand to her mouth as if she could still feel the imprint of Jerry's lips on hers. She smiled. Whatever happened in the future she would always have the memory of those blissful moments in his arms.

Chapter Thirteen

It was Christmas Eve and before they'd had a chance to finish their porridge, Mrs Andrews was chivvying the kitchen maids to get on. As they pushed their chairs back and hurried to do her bidding, Mr Phelps cleared his throat. Ruby paused, wondering what announcement he was going to make this morning. He did love to sound important.

'When I was ironing the master's newspaper this morning,' he said, 'I just happened to notice…'

Mrs Andrews laughed. 'Happened to notice? Come now, Mr Phelps, we all know you read the master's paper before you take it up to him.'

Hetty Catchpole gave her a withering look. 'Never mind that. Go on, Mr Phelps, what interesting news did you read of today?'

'Well, as you know, Lord Jameson's house was burgled recently – and now it's happened again.' He paused and they all nodded, hanging on his every word.

'Who was it this time?' asked Mrs Andrews.

'One of the big houses over in Rattigan Square. Some very valuable silver was taken. The paper says that the police believe it was the same gang. They think the villains are getting inside information but they are confident they will soon be caught.'

Ruby remembered Jeremiah telling her the same thing. She looked round the table and the thought occurred to her that he might suspect one of the servants here at Exton House. Was that why he'd made friends with her – to try and find out about the people she worked with? The fleeting thought was dismissed in an instant as she remembered those passionate moments in his arms. Besides, when he was with her he'd never expressed an interest in any of the household. She felt in her apron pocket for the ribbon which she always carried with her. But, to her dismay, it wasn't there. She must have left it in her room.

Mrs Andrews was shaking her head. 'Let's hope they get them soon. We're lucky Exton House has been spared - so far. Just think of her ladyship's jewels, and all that silver in the dining room.'

'It isn't just luck,' the butler said. 'It is due to our vigilance. I always make sure the house is secure before I retire for the night and in addition, Archie and Silas take turns to stay awake and listen out for any unusual sounds. We shall continue to do so until these villains are caught.'

They're not that vigilant, Ruby thought, remembering the window she'd found open the other day. She was about to mention it, but when she saw Mrs Catchpole glaring at her, she decided not to draw attention to herself. She picked up the dishes and hurried into the scullery.

As she rushed around trying to obey Mrs Andrews's commands as quickly as possible, she wished she was still working with Fanny preparing the rooms for the guests. Since Polly had come she was seldom needed to help upstairs.

Perhaps she would have a chance for a quick chat with her friend when she took the cans of hot water up for the visitors' baths. She'd have to be careful to keep out of Mrs Catchpole's way. Since finding her in the cellar that night, she had lost no opportunity of finding fault with her.

When the guest room bell jangled, she picked up the heavy can and started up the back stairs. At the top she saw Polly, who was getting fresh sheets from linen closet at the end of passage.

To her dismay, she saw that a pile of sheets was on the floor and Polly was on the verge of tears. 'I pulled one out and they all fell down,' she wailed.

Ruby set the can down on the floor and rushed to help her pick them up. 'Don't worry, can't be helped,' she said.

She picked up one sheet and began to fold it but at that moment Mrs Catchpole appeared.

The housekeeper's lips were set in the familiar tight grimace and she shoved the sheet into Polly's hands. 'This is disgraceful. Such slovenly behaviour. Tidy it up at once,' she snapped.

Then she rounded on Ruby. 'And what are you doing up here? Get on with your own work.'

Ruby bent to pick up the hot water can, hoping it wouldn't be cold by the time she reached the guest room. Before she could hurry away, Mrs Catchpole called her back. 'I suppose you're too taken up with your dalliance with the master's son to attend to your work properly. Well, it won't do, miss.'

Shocked, Ruby tried to explain, hoping that Polly had not heard the accusation. 'But it's not like that. He was the one who…' she stammered.

'They all say that. It takes two you know.' Hetty folded her arms across her bony chest and stood tapping her foot. 'I thought you'd learned your lesson. But no - now he's buying you trinkets and fripperies.'

'I don't know what you mean, Mrs Catchpole.'

'Oh, no?' She delved into her apron pocket and pulled out a length of red ribbon, waving it under Ruby's nose. 'Don't tell me you bought this out of your wages. You haven't been paid this quarter yet. So if Mister Oliver didn't give it to you, you must have stolen it.'

'But I didn't.' Ruby reached out to take the precious ribbon from her but the housekeeper snatched it away, a small smile on her lips. 'I'll be hanging on to this and if you don't behave yourself in future, the mistress shall hear of it.'

Ruby began to cry. Why didn't she believe her? Was she going to be dismissed?

Mrs Catchpole caught hold of her arm and shook her, pinching hard enough to leave a bruise. 'Stop snivelling girl. I'll take your word you're not a thief – this time,' she said. 'Just do your work and we'll say no more about it, but just step out of line and it'll be the worse for you.' She released Ruby abruptly and left her, saying, 'And don't come crying to me when you get into trouble.'

Ruby leaned against the wall, her limbs shaking. Mrs Catchpole had known all the time that it was Mister Oliver who had got her into trouble so why hadn't she tried to put a stop to it? Ruby knew the answer to the last question. After all, Hetty Catchpole was a servant like she was and, like her, must fear for her job if she tried to speak up about anything.

She took a deep breath and entered the guest room where Fanny was making up the bed, assisted by Polly.

'What's wrong –Mrs C been getting at you again?' Fanny asked.

Ruby was tempted to confide in her friend, but she couldn't say anything in front of Polly. She just shrugged and said, 'She always on at me.'

'You've been crying. What did she say to you?' Fanny asked.

'Just the usual – I don't know why she's picking on me all the time.'

'She had a go at me too.'

Fanny shook her head. 'Best get on with our work and try to keep out of her way,' she said.

They knew that the housekeeper was a bad-tempered old misery who didn't get on with anyone. She had got worse lately and seemed to delight in picking on all the servants, but she treated Ruby worst of all. The only one she had a good word for was Silas – and he was her nephew, Ruby remembered.

Mrs Catchpole went downstairs, smiling. She patted the piece of red ribbon in her pocket. Perhaps Mister Oliver had given it to Ruby in exchange for favours received. More likely she had stolen it on one of her errands to the market. Either way, she would hang on to it for now.

She went downstairs, confident that if that policeman turned up again asking questions, Ruby would be too scared to talk about the open window – a window which should have been firmly closed when Mr Phelps did his nightly round.

Hetty had been in service all her working life and she hated it – hated having to defer to her so-called betters, pretending subservience to the mistress of the house. Since she'd risen to the position of housekeeper her life had been a little better, especially now that she was the one giving the orders. But she longed for a home of her own, a little cottage by the seaside in the town where she'd grown up and where she and her sister could live out their lives in comfort, far from the smoke and grime of the city.

Thanks to her money-making sidelines, her savings had grown steadily and now, her goal was in sight. With her share from last night's break-in she would have enough to retire on.

Downstairs she hurried along the passage and out of the back door. She shivered, wishing she'd put her shawl round her. But she hadn't wanted anyone to realise she was going outside. Grateful for the fog which swirled around her, concealing her actions, she crept along close to the wall until she reached the window to the storeroom. She breathed a sigh of relief. Anyone passing would think it was closed, although when she tested it she could tell it wasn't securely fastened from the inside. She bent to put her face close to the glass and peered in. Yes, the stuff was there. It was safe enough for the time being. No one in the household should have any reason to go in there.

Hetty's lips tightened as she remembered that nosy girl poking around last night. Why was she getting coal at that time of night? It wasn't her job. She should talk to Mrs Andrews about that. Perhaps not. She didn't want to draw attention to herself.

She was about to sidle back into the house when she heard heavy footsteps. The figure of a man passed by the open gate and she shrank back, holding her breath. A gust of wind parted the tendrils of fog and she recognised the big policeman as the one who'd been to the house investigating the burglaries. She hugged the wall as the footsteps halted. She could see the man's dim outline through the mist and she held her breath as he turned, peering behind him, head on one side as if he were listening. He stood there for what seemed an age. Then he shrugged and walked on.

Hetty gave a sigh of relief as the footsteps faded into the distance. She waited until he'd turned the corner then, on impulse she took Ruby's ribbon from her pocket, dropping it on the ground under the window. If the police investigated, and if it was found, no one would believe the girl hadn't dropped it herself. At least it would divert suspicion from anyone else in the household. Hetty hurried indoors, hoping no one had noticed her absence.

At last the long day was over and, as Ruby said goodnight to Fanny, she envied her friend being able to go across to the stables and join her family at their supper. She pictured them sitting round the table in their apartment, chatting and laughing, their faces aglow in the gaslight.

As she sat at the table no one looked up to greet her and Mrs Andrews silently passed the dish of stew to her. It had been made from leftovers from their employers' dinner and the cook had bulked it up with big floury dumplings and extra vegetables. It was delicious and nourishing but Ruby could hardly manage a few mouthfuls.

She looked round at the other servants. Mrs Andrews was tucking in with her usual gusto; Mr Phelps never had much to say unless it was to reprimand one of the footmen or to lecture them all about something he'd read in the newspaper. Jimmy ate as if he didn't know where his next meal was coming from and Polly, who seldom spoke to anyone, had her head bent over her meal. Annie and Kitty, who usually chatted and giggled all the time, were also silent this evening.

Only Hetty and Silas were talking in low voices but Ruby couldn't help hearing when Silas raised his voice to say, 'I've told you, Aunt Hetty, I'll go and see her on my next day off. I can't just go out whenever I want to. You get more time off than I do, why don't you go?'

Ruby quickly looked down at her plate when she saw Hetty glaring at her. She guessed they were talking about the sick relative that the housekeeper had been visiting back in the autumn. Perhaps it was the worry about whoever was so ill that was making her so bad-tempered these days. Still, Ruby thought, she should be grateful she had a family to worry about. Just lately she'd been feeling the lack of any kin of her own to care about. But then she thought of Jerry and a warm flush stole over her. Even if they could never be together, the knowledge that someone loved her was enough to lift her spirits.

Appetite regained, she finished her stew and pushed her plate away. But even when the meal was done, work wasn't finished for the day. But, as she reached for her rough apron, ready to go upstairs and bank down the fires in the drawing room and library, empty the ashtrays and tidy the cushions, Mrs Andrews called her back.

What now, Ruby thought. Jimmy had already brought the coal up so she wouldn't have to go down to the dark cellar tonight.

She sighed. 'Yes, Mrs Andrews?'

'Ruby, love, I meant to ask one of you earlier. I'll need that extra big fish kettle tomorrow. Could you fetch it from the store room now so that Annie can give it a good clean first thing?'

Ruby nodded unwillingly and fetched a candle, remembering the last time she'd been sent to fetch something. She opened the door and looked across to the little window, relieved that this time it seemed to be firmly closed. She spotted the fish kettle on the top shelf and tried to reach it. But it was too high and she looked round for something to stand on.

That wooden crate would do, she thought. She set the candle on a small table and pulled it towards her. As she did so she heard a clink and something fell down behind the box. Dreading she had broken something, she took the candle and held it closer. It was a bundle of old sacking. She carefully unwrapped it, gasping as the candlelight revealed a pair of ornate silver candlesticks and a rose bowl. Wrapped in with them was a smaller bundle. Ruby carefully unrolled the linen tea cloth which clinked as a number of silver teaspoons fell out. In her time at Exton House she could not recall ever seeing these things before. She sat back on her heels and shone the candle over them. The candlesticks were beautiful, far more delicately-wrought than the ones on the sideboard in the Prestons' dining room. Why did they not use these? she wondered. Why were they hidden away down here?

The answer came to her in a flash of understanding. That was why the window had been left open the other night. She should tell someone. But who? Could someone in the household be in league with the gang? Her first thought was that Mrs Catchpole was responsible, although she and the other maids had often speculated about what the housekeeper got up to on her frequent absences, Ruby couldn't bring herself to believe that she was really part of a gang of burglars.

No, she would speak to Jerry next time she saw him - until then she would keep quiet, she decided.

Quickly wrapping the things again, she thrust the package behind the pile of crates, took the fish kettle from the shelf and hurried out into the passage, gasping as a figure appeared in front of her.

'What are you up to, Ruby?' Silas asked.

'Nothing,' she stammered. 'I'm just fetching this for Mrs Andrews.' She showed him the fish kettle and tried to pass him but he gripped her wrist, squeezing so that she almost dropped the candlestick.

'You shouldn't be creeping about down here at this time of night,' he said, grinning. 'The burglars might get you, knock you on the head like they did old Joe across the way.'

Ruby stood her ground. She wasn't going to let him see how frightened she was. Thrusting out her chin she said, 'You don't scare me, Silas James. Anyway, I could ask you why you're creeping around when everyone else is in bed.'

'I'm just doing my job – making sure the house is secure.' He let go of her and gave her a little push. 'Get away with you – and don't let me see you down here again.'

'You don't scare me,' she muttered once more. But he did. She was terrified as a terrible suspicion crept into her head. It must be Silas who was in league with the gang, not his aunt Hetty.

She couldn't get up to her room fast enough and she hastily pushed the chest against the door before falling into bed. And this time it wasn't Oliver Preston she was desperate to keep out.

* * *

Morning had come at last and Jeremiah was looking forward to the end of his shift and a well-deserved sleep at the station house. It had

158

seemed like a quiet night but a blanket of fog had crept up from the river - perfect cover for villains bent on mischief. The fact that it was Christmas would not stop them.

Rounding the corner of Warwick Square he stopped, sure he'd heard a noise. He stood for a few moments, listening but, deciding it had just been a cat, he walked on. Any villains who'd been abroad last night would be back in their beds by now, he thought. And that's where he was headed after just one more turn round the square. But he stayed alert all the same.

Back at the police station, Inspector Higgins beckoned him into his office. Heart thumping Jeremiah closed the door and stood to attention. Constables were only called into the office when they'd done something wrong but Jeremiah was sure he wasn't guilty of any misdemeanour. He hoped there hadn't been another burglary while he was on duty. But he consoled himself with the knowledge that the criminals were well aware of the beats the constables took and timed their break-ins accordingly. But remembering that odd noise he'd heard, he wondered if perhaps he should have investigated further. It was too late now, he thought, as he waited apprehensively for the inspector to speak.

Higgins had picked up a sheet of paper and silently contemplated it for a few nerve-wracking moments.

Jeremiah felt as if he'd been standing at attention for hours and was longing to shift his feet when the inspector gave a little cough and looked up.

His rather severe features relaxed into a smile and he said, 'Congratulations, Constable Locker – or should I say Sergeant Locker? You've been promoted. Well done.' He stood up and held out his hand for Jeremiah to shake.

'Thank you, sir,' the young man gasped, gripping his superior's hand. 'Thank you.' He didn't know what else to say.

'Well, lad, better get yourself down to the supply room for your new uniform.'

'Yes, sir.' Jeremiah stammered. He still hadn't quite taken it in. He had never dreamt that the longed-for promotion would come through so quickly. What a marvellous Christmas present, he thought. He'd have to write to his parents as soon as possible – they would be so proud.

'Start your new duties first thing tomorrow, early shift.' With a wave of his hand Inspector Higgins dismissed him.

After being fitted for the new uniform tail coat with its stripes on the arm, Jeremiah went back to the station house where he lodged with his fellow policemen. There was no one about – those not out on the beat were all in the canteen enjoying a special Christmas dinner. The beer would be flowing plentifully. They were not allowed to drink normally but Christmas Day was an exception.

Jeremiah didn't feel like joining them. Although he got on well with his fellow police officers, he suspected they secretly mocked him for his ambitions and he wasn't in the mood for their teasing today. He lay down on his bunk and contemplated the future, reflecting how different his life was now from the one he'd left behind in Norfolk.

Not for the first time, he dreamed of having his own home with Ruby there to welcome him at the end of his day's work. It was several weeks since he'd last seen her and he wondered if she was thinking of him. Perhaps she was enjoying celebrating Christmas with her friends at Exton House and was too busy to spare a thought for him.

In some ways the job was very similar. As assistant gamekeeper to his father on the Thorleigh Estate he had used his country skills to deter and catch poachers on the squire's land. It was his job, even if sometimes he felt a sneaking sympathy for those villagers who were only trying to keep their families from starving. It was a similar situation here. Take that lad the other day for instance; he'd looked hungry and cold and Jeremiah had no doubt he'd been guilty. But to him, the boy was a victim of circumstances. It was the real villains he was after and his promotion to sergeant would further his ambition. If he carried on like this he would soon be out of uniform and joining the ranks of the detectives at Scotland Yard.

What a day it had turned out to be. This morning he had apprehended a couple of pickpockets – a devious pair who pretended to be husband and wife. The woman would pretend to faint, usually in a crowded shop or market place. As a curious crowd gathered, the "husband" would pretend to panic, grabbing at people and begging them to help his poor "wife". In the process, watches, silk handkerchiefs and purses would disappear into his capacious pockets. As she "recovered", the crowd would disperse and he would help her up, putting his arm around her and leading her to a cab.

Jeremiah had seen them doing their act once before and had been instantly suspicious. The "husband" had been a little too solicitous for someone who'd been bullying his "wife" as they came out of a public house a little earlier. He guessed it wouldn't be long before they tried the same trick again and sure enough, he'd seen them performing in the street this morning. He had grabbed the man and swung his rattle to summon help. Both were now in custody loudly protesting their innocence.

Excitement about his promotion made him restless and, although he had the rest of the day off, he couldn't settle. He wanted to share his news with someone and he sat down and wrote to his parents. He knew they missed him and wished he had stayed in Thorleigh. But they understood why he'd left and were proud of him. They would be even prouder when they got the news of his promotion. He could imagine his mother telling her friends, 'My son's a sergeant now'.

He sealed the letter, left the station house and strolled towards the market. A cold bright sun brightened up the drab surroundings lending a false cheerfulness to the shabby streets. He crossed the road, trying to avoid the steaming piles of horse dung, jingling some coins in his pocket but as it was Christmas day the shops were shut. He wanted to buy a present for Ruby although he was trying to resist the temptation to spend his hard-earned wages. He was saving every penny so that one day he'd be able to move into his own place and ask Ruby to marry him.

An involuntary smile curved his lips as he imagined his own home and the girl he hoped to share it with. Now that he was a sergeant he was really in a position to go courting. Ruby was never far from his thoughts and he wished he could share his news with her. He hadn't seen her since their walk in the park. Had she really told him she loved him? Sometimes he wondered if he'd dreamt the whole thing. But then common sense reasserted itself. She was a servant, tied to the whim of her employers and that dragon of a housekeeper. She couldn't come and go as she pleased and, like many in her position, he knew she would be in trouble if it was suspected that she had "follower" as they were called.

He would just have to trust to luck and another chance encounter. If he walked past Exton House often enough, he was sure to catch sight of her soon. Firmly, he turned his steps away from the teeming streets towards Warwick Square.

Chapter Fourteen

'You all right, Ruby?' The small voice roused her and she opened her eyes to see Kitty standing over her, a candle wavering in her hand. Was it night time already? She sat up quickly, gasping as the room began to sway.

'That cough sounds real bad,' Kitty whispered. 'Can I do anything for you?'

'Sorry I woke you. My throat's so dry.'

'I'll go down to the kitchen and make you a hot drink,' Kitty offered.

'Thanks, but don't get caught. I don't want you to get into trouble,' Ruby said.

'Don't worry. They're all asleep.' Kitty disappeared and returned a few minutes later back with a steaming cup of tea. She sat on the side of the bed. 'You do look a bit pale, I must say,' she said. 'Do you need a doctor?

Ruby gave a weak laugh. 'I'd have to be dying before Mrs Catchpole would agree to call the doctor,' she said. 'No, I'll probably be all right by morning.'

'I hope so – it's Christmas Day don't forget.'

Christmas was the last thing on Ruby's mind. She couldn't stop thinking about what she'd found in the store room. She was sure it was worrying about it that had made her feel ill but she couldn't say anything to Kitty. But who could she tell? She daren't trust anybody.

As she finished the drink and lay down, Kitty glanced across at Annie who was already snoring. 'She don't seem worried about burglars tonight, does she?' She gave a little laugh and looked at Ruby earnestly. 'I know that's not why you bar the door, Rube. But you don't have to worry tonight. He won't be back till new year's'.

Ruby knew she was referring to Oliver. 'I know,' she said, 'but...'

Kitty gave a little giggle. 'I'll tell you who is creeping about when everyone else is in bed - Silas. He must have sneaked out to see a lady friend or something. He was coming in the back door when I was making your tea. I was going to try and make him jump but I didn't think he'd see the joke. He can be a bit moody sometimes.' She said goodnight, blew out the candle and got into bed.

As she drifted off to sleep it occurred to Ruby that there always seemed to be someone wandering about the house when they were all supposed to be asleep. Seeing lights on should deter the burglars though, she thought.

Ruby woke feeling much better although she hadn't had much sleep, waking every so often with a pounding heart. Silas had really scared her and the more she thought about it, the more she became convinced that he had had no business being down in the basement so late at night. Her suspicions had been strengthened when

Kitty said she had seen him too – ages after he'd told her he was off to bed himself?

She shook off the unsettling thoughts and made up her mind she would try to enjoy Christmas Day. Although the season meant extra work for them all, especially those in the kitchen, Mrs Andrews tried to make sure that the maids had time to enjoy the day itself. And then there was the extra food, the little delicacies they never had the chance to eat in normal times. Ruby never ceased to be amazed at the amount that was sent up to the dining room, as well as what came back to the kitchen uneaten.

The highlight of the day came after morning prayers when the servants were given their Christmas gifts. The men had new boots and waistcoats and the women received new aprons and shawls. To Ruby's surprise the maids were each given an embroidered handkerchief.

'They're from us,' said Miss Charlotte, a faint flush staining her pale cheeks. 'See we've put your initials in the corner, so they won't get muddled up in the laundry.'

Ruby took hers and bobbed a curtsey. 'Thank you, Miss Charlotte, Miss Elizabeth. It's very pretty,' she said. The "R" was embroidered in blue with a little flower beside it. Her own sewing was very rudimentary and she wished she were able to do such delicate work. But then, she reflected, the young ladies had the time to perfect those skills, didn't they.

The brief interlude was soon over and then it was back to work until supper-time. After the weeks of preparation as well as the constant running up and down stairs to meet the demands of their employers, it was a relief to sit down at the end of Christmas Day and relax.

When they were all seated round the big kitchen table with plates of cold meat and stuffing, roast potatoes and parsnips, in front of them, Mr Phelps stood up and reached behind him to the dresser. With a flourish he produced a bottle of port, saying, 'The master wishes us all a merry Christmas and a happy new year.'

He filled the glasses and they all drank the toast. As the warm liquid slid down her throat, Ruby almost choked. It wasn't just the unaccustomed drink, more the thought that she was unlikely to enjoy a happy new year once Mister Oliver came home. He was due back in town for the New Year's Eve party which the Prestons always gave, and she was sure he would not have forgotten, nor forgiven, her for barring the door to him.

She looked across the table at Fanny and Archie who were so obviously enjoying each other's company while Mrs Andrews looked on indulgently. At least someone's happy, she thought, wondering what Jerry was doing now and if he was thinking of her.

* * *

Although he was not officially on duty, as he walked through the streets towards Warwick Square, Jeremiah was alert for unusual activity. But all was quiet. Most people were indoors enjoying the unaccustomed day with no work. Dusk had fallen and the glow of lamplight from the houses he passed threw shadows on the blinds.

He knew the peaceful scene could be deceiving. The festive season did not deter those bent on criminal activity. In fact it was an ideal time for the villains to go about their business when honest people might have let their guard down.

There was a hint of snow in the air and he shivered a little. Perhaps he should have stayed back at the station in the warm. But he walked on, remembering his encounter with Silas James. He clenched his fists. The man had hinted that he had an interest in Ruby and he pictured him sitting next to her in the servants' hall, leering and making suggestive remarks. He couldn't bear the thought and, although he knew it would do no good, he turned the corner towards Exton House. Perhaps he would be lucky and catch a glimpse of Ruby. If not, he would call on Williams at the stables on the pretext of bringing him up to date on the burglary investigation. It would be easy to slip Ruby's name into the conversation and find out how she was.

As he approached Exton House he looked up at the front of the building. The big windows were ablaze with light from the gas chandeliers and he could hear music and laughter. Was Ruby up there, scurrying round waiting on those people? He didn't like the thought and he pictured himself going up to the house and taking her away. A foolish thought, he knew, and he gave a little laugh.

He'd only just become sergeant and would have to carry on bunking at the station house with the constables for now. But one day, he vowed, he would be in a position to marry and then he would ask Ruby to be his wife.

He glanced down into the basement area to see a faint glow from behind the curtained window but all was quiet and there was no sign of Ruby, not that he'd really expected to see her. He walked to the corner hoping that the gate to the stable yard would be open. He'd enjoy a chat with Williams. But no doubt the coachman too was inside in the warm, enjoying Christmas dinner with his family.

He was about to turn away when the small side gate opened and a figure slipped through. He almost called out thinking it was the coachman but something in the man's furtive manner stopped him. He stepped round the corner and waited until the man, whom he now recognised as Silas James, the footman at Exton House, had passed.

Following at a discreet distance, he realised that Silas was making for the warren of narrow streets down by the river. He quickened his steps to close the gap between them. He couldn't see if he was carrying anything and besides, he had no reason to accost the man. He had merely left his legitimate place of employment on a day that was a holiday for many people. He would probably say that he'd been given leave to visit his mother who, Jeremiah remembered, lived in one of these side streets.

Inspector Higgins would no doubt remind him that he had no grounds for suspecting Silas. So, Jeremiah thought, I'll just watch and wait until I do have grounds. And he was sure that if he were patient, he would catch the man out.

Silas had reached his mother's house and Jeremiah decided that he really was just paying a Christmas visit home after all. But, as he was about to turn away, the door opened and the man he'd had seen Silas with before came out. They stood arguing on the doorstep and Jeremiah moved a little closer, trying to keep to the shadows, straining to hear what was being said.

'Just tell him, Aunt Hetty wants her share of the money and she's not prepared to wait much longer.' Silas took a small package from his coat pocket. 'These aren't too recognisable so you should be able to get rid of them easily enough. I'll be back for the gelt.'

'It's too dangerous to get rid of all the stuff just yet. We'll have to lie low for a bit longer,' the other man said.

'And that's another thing – we can't use the same place this time. I think one of the maids is getting suspicious.'

The other man gave a coarse laugh. 'Well, you'll know how to deal with her, won't you?'

Silas laughed too and clapped the other man on the shoulder. 'Yeah, don't worry about it.' He hurried away and Jeremiah slunk back into the shadows, holding his breath until the footman had passed him.

He could have gone back to the station house and enjoyed the rest of Christmas day. He wasn't on duty after all. But he couldn't just leave it and he returned to Exton House, watching as Silas slipped in by the side door.

He sighed. He still didn't have any proof, nothing that would convince the inspector at any rate. He started as a voice called out of the darkness and the light from a lantern flickered across his face. 'Oh, it's you, Constable.' Williams held the lantern a bit higher. 'Oh, sorry, I should have said Sergeant. Just noticed your stripes.'

'Just got them,' Jeremiah said.

'Congratulations,' Williams said.

'Why aren't you indoors with your family today? Trouble with the horses?'

'No. I thought I heard a noise just before you came along.' He lowered his voice. 'There's been some funny goings-on around here lately…'

'What sort of goings-on?' asked Jeremiah.

'Not sure, really. It's just, I'm often up at night with the horses, you know. And I've seen lights, heard voices. And since poor old Joe got knocked on the head some months ago, I've been keeping my eyes and ears open.'

'Have you seen anything suspicious?'

Williams thought for a moment. 'Well, a couple of weeks ago, I noticed that little window was open and everything's supposed to be locked up tight at night time.' He pointed across the yard although in the darkness there was nothing to see.

'Show me,' Jeremiah said.

Williams held up the lantern and walked across to where a small window was set into the wall almost at ground level. 'See, where the paint is flaking. You can see it's been opened recently.'

'Did you report it?'

Williams shook his head. 'When I looked in the morning it was closed and to be honest I forgot all about it. Besides, I didn't think it was that important – it's too small for a burglar to get through.'

'Too small for a burglar but not for a small child. That's what they do these days you know – put a little lad through the window and get him to either open a door from inside or pass the stuff out to them.'

'But this house hasn't been robbed has it?'

Jeremiah thought for a moment. He took the lamp and knelt down, peering through the window. The light reflected off the window and it was hard to see what was inside. 'Some sort of storeroom,' he said, getting up. As he did so, the light caught something lying on the ground. He picked it up, suppressing an exclamation as he saw what it was. Handing the lantern back to Williams, he thrust the ribbon into his coat pocket.

Ruby had also noticed Silas leaving the celebrations. He and his aunt had been whispering together when he had suddenly stood up and, with a muttered oath, he had flung out of the room.

Mrs Andrews looked round, her face redder than usual from the port she had been drinking. 'What's up with him?' she asked.

'I told him it was about time he went to see his mother. My poor sister's not well, you know,' Hetty replied. 'He only visits when I nag him into it.'

'He's not gone out now, has he?'

Mr Phelps said, 'I gave him permission. Those who are fortunate enough to have family should not neglect them at Christmastide.'

Ruby thought about Fanny who was even now enjoying her festive supper with her parents and small brothers in their rooms above the stables. Would she ever have a home and family of her own, she wondered.

The party began to break up after Silas had gone and the maids dispersed to finish their evening chores. Ruby was setting out the trays for the morning when Mr Phelps came back from his usual round of the house securing doors and windows.

'Still up, Mrs Catchpole?' he asked.

'I thought I'd wait up for Silas. I'll lock the side door behind him if you like,' she replied.

'I'll wait with you,' the butler said. 'We can have another glass of that delicious port.'

Ruby was disappointed. With Silas out of the way, she had hoped to have a quiet word with Mr Phelps when everyone else had gone to bed. The bundle of silver she had discovered in the storeroom had been playing on her mind. She was sure now that it was the proceeds of the recent burglary. She found it to hard to believe that Silas was involved but he'd been really angry when he'd caught her coming out the storeroom. At the time she'd been quite frightened. She felt that she ought to tell someone her suspicions, but who could she trust? She had almost blurted it out to Mrs Catchpole until she remembered that she was Silas's aunt.

The housekeeper caught her eye as she lingered in the kitchen doorway and snapped, 'What are you hanging about for? If you've finished your work, be off to bed with you.' She followed the butler into his room, carrying the port bottle.

When they'd closed the door, Ruby waited for a moment, listening to the low murmur of their voices. She'd risk it, she decided, darting down the passageway to the storeroom. She had to see if the stuff was still there. If it had gone, she would say nothing. She wouldn't be able to prove it had ever been there after all. But if it was, she would make an opportunity to slip out of the house tomorrow and try to find Jerry. He would know what to do.

She daren't light a candle so she left the kitchen door open to provide a little light. She opened the door to the storeroom and felt her way across to the dark corner where the sacking bundle had been hidden. There it was. Cautiously she unrolled it. Two candlesticks and a bowl. But where were the spoons? There had been four or five teaspoons when she'd looked before. Someone had been here since her last visit. Now she was sure they were stolen goods. Whoever was responsible for hiding the stuff had taken some of it away – to sell, she supposed. It could only be Silas, she thought, and Mrs Catchpole was in on it too. That was why they'd been arguing at the supper table. Perhaps the housekeeper was impatient for her share of the money.

Ruby tried to think of another explanation for their behaviour but at heart she knew Hetty Catchpole's sister was not as sick as she made out. Visiting her was just an excuse to get away from Exton House.

The noise of a door closing startled her and she held her breath, shrinking back behind the half open door. She heard Silas's voice and then Mrs Catchpole asked loudly, 'How did you find my poor sister tonight?'

There was low murmur in reply and Mr Phelps asking if the side door was locked securely. Then they all wished each other a good night and the gas lamp in the kitchen was turned off.

Ruby waited a few moments until she was sure that all was quiet before, trembling with fright, she crept along the dark passage, felt her way across the kitchen and mounted the backstairs to her room. Tomorrow, she must find a way to slip out and find Jerry. She prayed that he'd be able to reassure her, tell her that her fears were the result of an over-active imagination. But if he agreed that something fishy was going on, he was the person to deal with it.

Chapter Fifteen

After the frantic busyness of the Christmas celebrations, life at Exton House settled back into its normal routine. The Bramptons and their attendant servants had departed and to Ruby's relief Oliver had gone with them.

As Mrs Andrews had remarked when they finally left, it certainly wasn't from a desire to spend more time with his fiancée. The hunting season was in full swing and Mister Oliver had more love for his horses then he had for Miss Amelia.

There was to be no slacking for the servants though. Mrs Catchpole continued to chivvy the maids and make snap inspections of their work and they still had to keep on their toes. But there wasn't the frantic activity which had sent Ruby to bed exhausted each night.

Ruby hadn't been sleeping well since her discovery in the basement, but exhaustion had finally sent her into a deep slumber. She felt as if she'd only just drifted off when she woke with thudding heart to someone shaking her roughly by the shoulder.

Frantic, she pushed the hand away, whimpering until she realised it was Kitty, urging her to hurry up. Morning had come already and she had overslept.

'I'll only be a minute,' she said, jumping out of bed and beginning to dress. As the events of the previous night came back to her, she began to shake, her fingers fumbling with the laces of her corset.

The door opened and Polly came in. 'Hurry up. The police are here,' she said, her voice trembling with excitement.

'What again?' Kitty exclaimed. 'What is it this time?'

Ruby was sure she knew and her heart raced as she followed Kitty downstairs. This must have something to do with the silver candlesticks and other things she'd found hidden away. Perhaps she should have spoken up sooner. If Jerry was one of the policeman she vowed to be brave and speak out.

Downstairs a large uniformed police constable stood guard outside the kitchen door. 'Inside, you two. The inspector is with Sir Charles in his study. He wants to question you all in turn. Meantime none of you is to leave the house,' he said.

'What's happened?' Ruby asked.

'You'll find out soon enough,' he replied, turning to Polly. 'Is that all the servants now?'

She nodded.

Entering the kitchen Ruby looked at the stunned faces assembled round the table. She went and put her arm round Annie who'd also been crying. Hetty Catchpole sat with folded arms, a grim set to her lips.

'Have we been burgled?' Ruby asked.

The housekeeper shot her a malevolent glance. 'Not us – next door,' she snapped. 'They

179

seem to think someone in this household is involved.'

Ruby sank into a chair at the table, wondering why Mrs Catchpole had directed the remark at her in particular. Did she think that Ruby suspected her nephew's involvement and was she warning her to keep quiet?

The other servants seemed stunned, sitting in silence, but Mrs Andrews thumped her fist on the table. 'It's ridiculous. How could they think such a thing?' Her face reddened with indignation. 'Anyway, that's no reason to sit around looking like a wet week in July. There's still work to be done.' She started chivvying the kitchen maids to get ready to serve the breakfasts. 'Sir Charles won't want his till the police are finished but her ladyship and the misses are already in the dining room. This has put the whole household in a dither.'

She started crashing pots and pans around, a sure sign she was upset and the kitchen maids scurried to do her bidding. 'I don't know why they need to talk to us. We don't know anything,' she said, banging the iron kettle down on the range.

'They're only doing their duty,' Mr Phelps said. 'I feel sure no one in this household knows anything. We were all kept too busy yesterday, serving the family and enjoying our own Christmas celebrations, to notice what might have been happening next door.'

'Silas – you went out after supper. Did you see anything?' Kitty piped up.

'No, I didn't,' he replied shortly.

'I was still up when he came back – so was Mr Phelps,' Hetty Catchpole said.

The butler nodded. 'I'm sure you'd have told us if you'd seen anyone lurking in the square.'

The conversation ended abruptly as the door opened and a police constable beckoned to Hetty. 'Mrs Catchpole, the inspector will see you in Sir Charles's study now.'

She wasn't gone long. When she came back, Silas said, 'Finished with you already, Auntie? They haven't arrested you then.'

He laughed and she snapped back. 'It's no joke, Silas. I just told them that as far as I knew no one except you left the house last night. I'm sure none of us could possibly be involved with this gang they were talking about. I don't think they have any grounds for their suspicions but I suppose they're getting desperate to arrest somebody. Nearly every house in the square has been robbed and they must be wondering why Exton House has been spared.'

Ruby felt herself blushing as the housekeeper looked straight at her. Had she too seen the parcel of silver in the storeroom and jumped to the conclusion that Ruby had put it there? It was a reasonable assumption after all as Hetty had seen her in the storeroom closing the window. Had she told the police?

'You're right, Mrs Catchpole,' Mrs Andrews said. 'You can understand them being suspicious.'

181

'Well, we can only tell the truth, can't we?'

Ruby lowered her eyes to hide her apprehension. She didn't want to get anyone into trouble but she would tell the truth if it looked as if they suspected her of anything.

The policeman called Kitty next and when she'd left the room, Ruby offered to take the trays to the dining room. Anything was better than sitting around waiting. At the bottom of the stairs, Silas approached her. 'Have they spoken to you yet?' he asked.

She shook her head.

'I don't know why they're questioning the servants,' he said. 'We don't know anything, do we?'

She trembled at the look he gave her 'I certainly don't,' she said, trying to push past him.

His hand shot out and gripped her arm. 'I'm not so sure about that,' he said. 'Still, I'm sure you'll do the right thing. Remember, my aunt knows something about you – something I'm sure you wouldn't want your policeman friend to know about.'

Ruby gasped. She had been certain no one in the Preston household knew of her meetings with Jerry.

Silas grinned and twisted her wrist so viciously that she nearly dropped the tray. He let go suddenly and she walked away quickly. She wouldn't let him see how upset she was.

When she returned from the dining room Mr Phelps told her that she was next to be questioned. She mounted the stairs to Sir Charles's study with dry lips and a pounding heart. Would she be brave enough to tell the police inspector about the hidden hoard of silver?

* * *

Jeremiah should have been pleased that at last his suspicions of Silas James were being taken seriously. As soon as they had heard of the bungled break-in at the house next door in the early hours of this morning, he had approached Inspector Higgins and told him of his talk with Williams, the coachman, and how he had followed Silas on several occasions.

'He may tell us he is visiting his old mother down in Whitechapel but he also has some rather shifty-looking acquaintances in that area,' he reminded his superior.

Now he waited apprehensively for Ruby to be called in to the study. He knew in his heart that she had nothing to do with it but Inspector Higgins was convinced that one of the maids could have been involved. 'Some of these simple girls will do anything for a young man who takes their fancy,' he had said.

And then there was that red satin ribbon lying on the ground beside the little window. Ruby would have had no valid reason for being in that part of the yard. It seemed too much of a coincidence that someone else would have a similar piece of ribbon, especially as Ruby had told him they weren't allowed to have such colourful adornments.

If only he hadn't mentioned his suspicions, he thought, no one would have connected this household with the crime. But duty had compelled him to report what he had discovered. And now, here he was, wondering how he could protect the girl he loved without compromising his principles.

She came in hesitantly and looked across at him but he avoided her eyes.

'The inspector just wants to ask a few questions, miss,' he said.

Inspector Higgins cleared his throat. 'You know what we're investigating don't you?'

Ruby nodded.

'We just want to know if you've seen or heard anything that would help us to catch these criminals.'

Once again Ruby's eyes flicked towards Jeremiah and he held his breath. But she stood up straighter and her chin jutted. 'I don't know anything, sir.'

Sir Charles shifted in his seat. 'Is all this questioning really necessary? I don't see how upsetting my servants and keeping them from their work is going to help.'

Jeremiah pursed his lips. Typical of the upper class, he thought. Only thinking of their convenience. If Sir Charles had his way, this would all be kept quiet.

The inspector apologised. 'But, Sir Charles, we are acting on information received and we must investigate and who knows, you could be next.' He turned to Ruby. 'All right, miss, you can go. Send in the next one.'

As she left, Ruby glanced at Jeremiah. He was tempted to smile encouragingly but he kept his face impassive. But in spite of finding the ribbon, he was sure she was not involved. At least that's what he told himself. Besides, his keen policeman's eye had noticed that she seemed nervous during the questioning and that she had rubbed at her wrist once or twice. As she'd left the room, she put up a hand to brush back a stray lock of hair and he had spotted the red marks. Had someone threatened her to keep quiet?

While they waited for the footman to come up from the basement, Inspector Higgins said to Sir Charles. 'Perhaps you're right, Sir, but you have my word that anything we discover will not reflect on you or your family. I'll get through this as quickly as possible and I'm sorry your household has been disrupted.'

'So you should be. My son is getting married soon – a very influential family. I don't want them hearing about this.'

'We'll try to be discreet, sir,' the inspector said. 'However, we will have to search the house just in case the stolen goods are here.'

Sir Charles began to bluster but the Inspector assured him they would confine their searches to the lower regions of the house and the family's private apartments would not be disturbed. 'We do have a warrant, sir,' he said, proffering the sheet of paper which had been signed early that morning by a magistrate.

Jeremiah couldn't wait to start the search but they had to finish the interviews first.

The next servant to enter was Silas James and, before the inspector could speak, Sir Charles said, 'This is my housekeeper's nephew. He's been with us since he was a lad – worked his way up from boot boy and has never given any cause for complaint.'

Silas nodded. 'That's right, sir,' he said, addressing Inspector Higgins. 'I hate the thought of any scandal attaching itself to the Preston name. The family's been very good to me, sir.'

Jeremiah tried to keep his face impassive at the footman's obsequious manner. It was an effort not to interrupt and accuse the man. Why didn't the inspector do so, especially after what Jeremiah had told him.

'I'll take your master's word for it, then. But I do need to ask you where you went last night. You were seen leaving the house.'

Silas glanced at Sir Charles. 'Mr Phelps gave me permission, sir. I went to visit Ma – took her a Christmas present, didn't I?' He leaned towards the inspector. 'You can go and ask her if you don't believe me.'

'We may well do that.' The inspector nodded dismissal and Silas bowed and left the room.

He hadn't glanced at Jeremiah or shown any sign that they'd met before but as he opened the door he glanced over his shoulder, his lips twisted in an insolent smile.

Jeremiah had a job to hide his contempt. He wasn't so easily taken in. The man's obsequious manner revolted him. While they interviewed the rest of the servants, he only half listened. He couldn't get the thought of those red marks on Ruby's wrist out of his mind. Did she know more than she'd let on? When she'd entered the study he'd been pleased that she hadn't acknowledged him. If the inspector knew of their acquaintance it might prejudice his questioning of her. Now he wondered if she'd been afraid that whoever was threatening her would not take kindly to her being friendly with a policeman.

He decided that for the time being he would keep his suspicions to himself. He'd wait and see what the search revealed. He knew he should have mentioned finding the ribbon outside the basement window. It could be important evidence after all. But then, it might have nothing at all to do with the burglary. His feelings for Ruby warred with his sense of duty. He decided that if he could get her alone, he would give her the chance to explain.

Chapter Sixteen

I wish Fanny would stop talking about it, Ruby thought, as she cleared out the grate and polished the cast iron fire surround. They were all behind with their regular work as they hadn't been allowed to leave the kitchen until they'd all been questioned. They had been sent up from the basement regions to get on with work in other parts of the house and a constable stood guard at the green baize door leading to the kitchen regions while the search went on.

Ruby wondered what would happen when they found the stolen silver in the basement storeroom. Would Silas and Mrs Catchpole be arrested? She sincerely hoped so. Once they were safely locked up she wouldn't be afraid to tell he police what she had seen. Or would she?

Silas's threat to tell Jerry about her involvement with Oliver had really frightened her. Although she knew none of it was her fault and that she shouldn't be ashamed, she dreaded him knowing about it.

Her heart had raced at the sight of Jerry standing beside the police inspector so tall and smart in his uniform. It had taken her a moment to realise why he looked so different today until she noticed the different coat and the stripes on his arm. She was thrilled that he had been promoted to sergeant and wished she could say so. But of course he had pretended not to know her as he had on that earlier occasion when he came to question the servants. If only he had given just the smallest smile in her direction though.

Fanny was still going over the events of the morning, speculating as to why the police thought anybody at Exton House could be mixed up in something so wicked. 'Perhaps they think Mr Phelps is the gang leader,' she said with a giggle.

'Don't be silly, Fanny,' Ruby said, longing to tell her friend to drop the subject. Her head was pounding and the bruise on her wrist was throbbing, reminding her of Silas's threat. From the look in his eyes she had soon realised that he was quite capable of carrying it out.

'I'm only joking,' Fanny said, sounding offended. Ruby apologised and turned her face away, pretending to be intent on her polishing.

When they went down to the kitchen to fetch the water jugs, Mrs Andrews told them that the police had finished their search and left the house. The servants had been allowed back to work and Mrs Andrews was berating the kitchen maids as she was all behind with preparing the luncheon.

'I can't be doing with all this upset,' she said, thumping a lump of bread dough onto the kitchen table and pounding at it.

'Did they find anything?' Ruby asked anxiously.

'They wouldn't tell us, would they?' Mrs Andrews snapped.

Silas was there, lounging in a chair, and he shot a malevolent glance at Ruby. 'Let's hope they haven't – it'll be the worse for someone in this household if they do,' he said.

Mrs Andrews rounded on him, her wooden spoon waving threateningly in his face but before she could say anything, Mr Phelps intervened and sent Silas about his work.

'I think we should all try to carry on as normal,' he said.

* * *

The two sergeants followed Inspector Higgins into his office and took off their stove pipe hats. They stood at attention, waiting until he was seated behind his desk.

He looked up and said, 'Well, Harris, what developments?'

'We've found some of the stuff, sir,' he said, laying the parcel down on the desk.

When he unwrapped the sacking, two candlesticks rolled across the desk and Inspector Harris's eyes lit up. 'From the Rattigan Square robbery,' he said. 'And what's this?'

The white material was unrolled to reveal a maid's frilled apron wrapped around a small silver bowl. Jeremiah suppressed a gasp. So one of the maids was involved. But it couldn't be Ruby, he protested silently. He would stake his life that she was innocent of any involvement. But he was conscious of the length of red satin ribbon which he had picked up outside and which he still had in his pocket. Coupled with the apron and the way she had avoided his eyes during the interview this morning, it was hard to discount the evidence. It all added up and Jeremiah knew he should mention finding the ribbon. But he just couldn't bring himself to accuse her even if it did mean compromising his principles.

At his exclamation Inspector Higgins looked up sharply. 'Yes, Locker, I agree. There's only one conclusion - despite Sir Charles's protests that none of his staff could be involved, I'm afraid the maids will all have to be questioned again – no matter what he says.' He spread out the apron on his desk, noting the blood stains. 'It looks as if she injured herself, perhaps climbing through the window.'

Jeremiah sighed with relief. He had never seen any cuts on Ruby's hands. The only injury he had noticed was the bruise on her wrist.

'Locker, you must go back to Exton House and demand of Sir Charles that all the maids be questioned again. One of them has been lying to us. Take a constable with you, Sergeant. You may have to make an arrest.'

The inspector dismissed them and Jeremiah beckoned to a constable to come with him. After explaining where they were going and why he relapsed into silence, clutching the parcel containing the damning evidence and desperately trying to convince himself that it couldn't be Ruby's apron. Perhaps it was but, remembering those bruises on her wrist, he wondered if Silas might have forced her to help him? He just couldn't believe that all the while she had walked along with him smiling and responding to his kisses, she had been deceiving him.

As he strode along, deep in thought, compassion overtook anger. He still had to face up to the facts though. Despite the possible extenuating circumstances, it was now obvious that the girl he'd fallen in love with was guilty of something.

* * *

With a final polish of the copper pan, Ruby made up her mind. She wasn't afraid of Silas James or Hetty Catchpole. What was worse after all - Jerry finding out what had happened between her and Mr Oliver or being accused of a crime in which she had no part?

She hoped that when the time came she would be brave enough to reveal her suspicions of the housekeeper and the footman. For, if Silas was guilty, his aunt must know about it and, if not actively involved, would try to shield him from the police investigation.

She would go to Lady Anne and ask her advice. She didn't trust any of the servants at the moment except for Fanny and she wouldn't be much help. She was on her way up to the drawing room to speak to her employer when a hand grasped her arm.

'I hope you're not thinking of doing something silly,' Silas whispered.

She whirled round to confront him and her eyes widened. 'Of course not', she stammered. 'Her ladyship sent for me to make up the fire.' Her voice shook and she could tell he didn't believe her.

He poked her in the chest with a bony finger and thrust his face close to hers. 'Just remember then. If me or my aunt get into trouble, it will be the worse for you.'

'I've done nothing to be ashamed of.'

'I'm not talking about what went on with the master's son and what happened in the cellar,' he said with a leer.

'I don't care who knows about that,' she lied. 'It wasn't my fault.'

'So you say but who will believe you. Anyway, you may not care about yourself, but what about your friend and her little brothers? You wouldn't want to see them hurt would you?'

'You wouldn't?' Ruby's knees buckled and the blood drained from her face.

'Just remember what I said – and think about those boys.' He walked away to answer the front door.

Still shaking, Ruby leaned against the wall trying to summon up her courage once more. She could hear Silas speaking to someone in the hall. 'You should have used the tradesman's entrance, Sergeant,' he said.

193

'I've no time for such niceties. Tell Sir Charles I must speak to him at once.'

Ruby recognised the voice. Today it seemed harsher than the soft Norfolk accent that had so enchanted her during their walks. Was it only a few weeks ago? Her heart sank. Why had he come back? Had they discovered something? If he questioned her again what would she say?

She stood in the passageway leading to the back stairs, her knees trembling, her heart racing. She had hidden in the shadows as Silas escorted the two policemen into the library and then slipped away before the footman could return to continue his threats. He was the least of her worries now. At any moment she expected to be summoned to the library to be questioned again.

But, despite her fear of Silas's threats she had made up her mind to tell the truth even if they didn't believe her.

* * *

Jeremiah's thoughts were in turmoil. Only he knew that the scarlet ribbon belonged to Ruby. He was sure she wouldn't have told anyone else about it. Should he speak up and admit his involvement with her? He had a feeling it wouldn't be wise. Inspector Higgins might not believe that he hadn't known her for long and that their friendship had only consisted of a few walks through the market and an afternoon in the park. What's more, if he admitted knowing her, they might take him off the case. He wouldn't be much help to her then. Despite the evidence, he was sure in his heart that she'd done nothing wrong.

Sir Charles was still blustering, trying to convince them that no one in his household would do such a thing. 'It's all nonsense. Mrs Catchpole is in charge of the servants and she keeps a very close eye on them.'

'But, Sir Charles, we have proof that someone in this house is receiving stolen goods and your footman has been seen in the company of some very undesirable characters,' Jeremiah said firmly.

'Nevertheless, you have no real proof. The gates are usually locked at night but I know they are sometimes left open, especially when my son is going to be late home. Anyone could have slipped into the stable yard and hidden the stuff here.'

'Then how do you account for this?' Jeremiah asked, pointing to the silver bowl and the item it was wrapped in. 'Mrs Catchpole has identified this apron as belonging to a maid in your household.'

'Not necessarily. I don't take much account of what my maids are wearing but it's a common enough design,' Sir Charles said dismissively. 'However, we will soon settle this.' He reached for the bell pull. 'I am sure my housekeeper has made a mistake. She will be able to tell you if any of ours are missing.'

While they waited in silence for Hetty Catchpole to answer the summons, Jeremiah had the irrational hope that she would set his mind at rest. She would tell him that the apron wasn't Ruby's. And after all, the ribbon could belong to one of the other maids - servant girls often spent their meagre wages on such fripperies.

The door opened and the housekeeper came in, her eyes respectfully lowered. She bobbed a curtsey and said, 'You wanted to speak to me, Sir Charles?'

'The sergeant wants to ask you some more questions,' Sir Charles said.

'Yes, sir.'

Jeremiah showed her the apron. 'Mrs Catchpole, you told us this apron belonged to one of your maids.'

She took it from him and examined it slowly. 'I'm not sure now, sir. It certainly looks like the style our housemaids wear.'

'Could you tell if any are missing from this house?'

'I haven't noticed, sir. I'd have to check. Some might be in the laundry.'

'Well, do so then. And let me know as soon as possible. In the meantime, I'll question the maids again.' Jeremiah waved a hand in dismissal. 'Send Ruby Hinton in.' He sighed. Best to get it over and done with. The housekeeper's doubts had raised fresh hope. But there was still that telltale ribbon to explain away.

* * *

Ruby had crept back to the hall to listen at the closed library door. She could hear Sir Charles's voice raised in anger but she couldn't make out what he was saying. She took her duster out of her apron pocket and pretended to polish one of the door knobs.

Hetty Catchpole was in there now. What did the police want with her? One thing was certain - she would never tell the truth and implicate herself. But she could accuse Ruby, safe in the knowledge that Silas's threats would stop her from revealing what she knew.

She hesitated, trying to decide if it was too late to run away. But where would she go? Approaching footsteps sent her scuttling away to hide behind a huge jardinière but Silas caught sight of her. 'I wonder what she's telling them in there? Sir Charles trusts her – he'll believe whatever she says.' His lips twisted in a malicious smile. 'Those two policemen will be taking you away any minute.'

'You know I had nothing to do with it,' Ruby protested.

He pushed her back against the wall, thrusting his face so close she could smell his foul breath. 'I don't know anything. Besides, who will they believe – a respected servant who's served this family for years, or a slut like you?'

She pushed past him. 'I don't care what you say, I'm going to tell the truth.'

He grasped her shoulder and spun her round. 'Do that and it will be the worse for you. And don't think you'll be safe even in prison. My aunt and I have friends everywhere.'

'I'm not afraid of you,' Ruby said defiantly. At that moment she was terrified but she would not let him see it.

'Maybe not.' He smiled that evil smile 'But don't forget what I told you. You wouldn't want anything bad to happen to that friend of yours, would you – or those two little brats over in the stables?'

Before she could reply, the library door opened and Hetty came out. 'They want to speak to you now, Ruby,' she said. She nodded at Silas. 'What's she been saying?'

'Don't worry, Aunt Hetty. She'll do the right thing.' He was still grasping her shoulder and he gave her a little shake. 'Won't you?' he hissed.

'I'm sure she will,' Hetty said, her eyes glittering coldly as they bored into Ruby's.

Silas released her and, trembling, she stumbled away from him and knocked on the library door.

Chapter Seventeen

Ruby stood in front of Sir Charles, her hands clasped in front of her, her eyes lowered. She dare not look at Jerry – Sergeant Locker as she must think of him now. It had already occurred to her that it might look bad for him if she was accused of anything and his superiors found out they knew each other.

Sir Charles addressed her kindly, so different from his son, she thought. 'I'm sure you can explain all this. Just tell the truth and you'll be all right.'

She nodded and he went on, 'Sergeant Locker is hoping you can help.'

'If I can, sir,' she whispered.

Jeremiah cleared his throat. 'As you must now be aware, we have discovered a quantity of stolen goods hidden in this house. We must find out who has been aiding the burglary gang.' He showed her the apron. 'Do you know who it belongs to?'

'It looks like one of mine, sir.' She picked it up, recognising it as her own from the bloodstains. She had finally managed to put that dreadful night out of her mind, but seeing the apron brought it all flooding back. Mrs Catchpole had said she would see to it and Ruby had assumed she had it in the laundry. She couldn't deny it was hers though. She nodded and handed the garment back.

'How did it get stained? Did you cut yourself?'

'I don't remember,' she said, feeling the blush stealing up her neck.

'Well, miss, can you explain how a silver bowl came to be wrapped in it – valuable item stolen from a house in Rattigan Square?'

'No – I don't know anybody in Rattigan Square.' She knew she sounded evasive but she was trying to think things through. Mrs Catchpole must have hung on to the apron and put it with the stolen goods to implicate her.

She should speak up as she had resolved to do – not that they would believe her. But the memory of Silas's vicious expression as he had threatened to harm Fanny's brothers made her shake her head in denial. She wasn't afraid for herself but she couldn't bear the thought of being responsible for little Alfie and his brother being hurt.

'It will go easier if you tell us what you know,' Jeremiah said. 'I'm sure you're not the only one involved. Someone must have forced you into it.'

She straightened her shoulders and looked him in the eye. 'I don't know anything. I can only tell you that I didn't put the stuff there.' That was true at least.

'Well, since you insist on shielding your accomplices, I have no recourse but to take you into custody. Perhaps you'll be willing to speak up when you've seen the inside of a cell.'

Ruby gasped at the coldness in his tone. She felt her knees begin to give way. How could Jerry treat her like this? Hadn't he said he loved her only a little while ago? And now he was speaking so harshly. Did he really believe her capable of such wrongdoing?

'Constable, a chair,' Jeremiah snapped. He helped her to sit and began to rub her hands. 'Now then, miss, I know it's a shock for you but you must realise I'm only doing my duty.' His voice had softened and, looking into his eyes, she realised that he wasn't happy about what he was doing.

Tears began to fall and she sobbed, 'I'm sorry, I can't tell you.' The tears flowed faster.

'Constable, ring that bell. Get someone to fetch her some water,' Jeremiah ordered.

As her sobs gradually subsided, Jeremiah asked, 'Are you ready to tell us what happened now?'

Ruby nodded and was about to speak when the door opened and Hetty came in.

'You rang, sir?'

'Give the girl some water,' Sir Charles barked.

She came over to where Ruby was sitting and handed her a glass. 'What have they been saying to you, dear? Are you all right?'

Her voice was kind but Ruby flinched beneath her malevolent gaze. She had so wanted to be brave, to tell the whole story. But she couldn't. 'They think I helped the burglars but it wasn't me.'

She started to cry again and Hetty took her hand. 'I'm sure they'll find out the truth, dear,' she said, squeezing Ruby's hand so hard that the knuckles cracked.

Sir Charles strode over to them and knocked the glass out of her hand. 'Get back to your work, woman,' he shouted. 'And you two, get this person out of my house. Take her away.'

Jeremiah helped Ruby up. 'I'm sorry, miss. We'll have to take you in,' he said. He sent the constable to fetch a cab and led her down the back stairs to the stable yard.

As the cab came through the gates, Kitty pushed past the other servants who had crowded in the doorway to witness her arrest. 'Here Rube, you might need this,' she said, pulling off her woollen shawl and thrusting it into Ruby's hand.

Ruby didn't have a chance to thank her as the constable pushed her up the step into the cab. Jeremiah followed and sat opposite her and the constable climbed up beside the driver.

Huddled into a corner, she closed her eyes, unable to face him. She hoped that he would say something, give her some sign that he believed her innocent. But he was silent for the whole journey to the police station. It was as if he had never laughed and joked with her, bought her a red satin ribbon, kissed her so passionately and told her he loved her.

If only she had managed to tell him of her suspicions before now. Better yet, that she had never let Silas and his aunt realise that she had found the stolen goods. But it was too late now. She really believed that she would not be safe from Silas even in prison. Besides, even if he couldn't hurt her personally, there was still Fanny and her two little brothers to worry about.

The carriage gave a jolt and Ruby sighed and opened her eyes to see Jeremiah staring at her intently. As the vehicle drew to a halt he leaned forward, took her hand, caressing her fingers which still smarted from Hetty's vicious grip and said, 'Just tell me one thing, Ruby. Were you a willing accomplice or did they make you help them?'

She snatched her hand away, her eyes blazing. 'No! I didn't do anything. Why don't you believe me?' She started to cry again.

'I want to, Ruby. But you must speak up,' he said. 'I can't help you if you don't talk to me.'

If he really wanted to help he would have accepted that she was innocent, she thought. But he had gone ahead and arrested her anyway. When the cab jolted to a halt and he went to help her down, she shrugged him off.

Chapter Eighteen

Ruby was hustled into a small bare room containing a table and one chair. She sat down and the constable took up a position near the door. Jeremiah stood over her. 'Is there anything you want to tell us before you're charged?' he asked.

Ruby had stopped crying now and she shook her head.

'We'll have to lock you up then,' he said. He nodded to the constable. 'I'll take her down to the cells. You go and report to Inspector Higgins.'

He took Ruby's arm and led her down a stone staircase to the cells below. The tiny room smelled damp and there was green mould on the walls. Grey light filtered through the barred window high up on one wall. Ruby shivered and pulled the shawl closer around her shoulders, grateful to Kitty, who had braved the housekeeper's displeasure to hand it to her as the policemen hustled her away.

She sank down on a narrow bunk which was bolted to the wall and looked up at Jeremiah. 'What's going to happen to me?'

'That depends on the charges – probably accessory. That means you agreed to help the thieves by hiding the stuff.' Now that they were alone his voice softened. 'Ruby, you must speak up – tell the whole story.'

She desperately wanted to confide in his but she dare not risk it. She shook her head. 'There's nothing to tell.'

'Oh, Ruby, my love, you don't know how much I want to believe you. But, the evidence…' He sighed 'If you didn't do it, who did? And how come the things were wrapped in your apron?'

Ruby tightened her lips and turned her head away. If only she could tell him – how Mrs Catchpole had covered up for her and promised to dispose of the blood-stained apron. It wasn't just the thought of Silas's threats that kept her quiet. How could she explain the bloodstains?

Jerry took her hand. 'I'm trying to help you, Ruby. If you change your mind about talking…'

The door opened and he dropped her hand as the constable entered. 'The inspector wants you, Sergeant,' he said.

Jeremiah straightened up. His voice changed and he said formally, 'Well, miss, you'll come up before the magistrate tomorrow. They'll read out the charges and ask how you plead, then set a date for your trial.' He went out, slamming the door shut.

The sound echoed down the bleak corridor and Ruby cringed as she heard the key turn in the lock. She lay down on the hard bunk and stared at the tiny window high above her. As night fell, the grey patch darkened and she closed her eyes. But sleep would not come. The thoughts whirled in her head. Did Jerry really want to help her? Should she have spoken up?

205

After all, who could hurt her here in this lonely cell? And if she told Jerry about Silas's threats he could warn Fanny's father to be on his guard. Surely the boys would be safe with their mother and father watching out for them.

At last she dozed, but she was woken often by shouts and curses from the other cells, the slamming of doors and the tramp of feet along the corridor.

As dawn light began to filter through the barred window, she heard the key in the lock and started up. Her bones ached from the cold, adding to her misery.

A woman with strands of straggly grey hair poking out from her bonnet came in. She put a dish of gruel and a mug of water down on the stool beside the bunk.

'Breakfast, dearie. Eat up. You'll not get anything else for a while.' She glanced behind her and spoke in a harsh whisper. 'My friend Silas said to remember what he said.' She left the cell and the door was locked once more.

Ruby cowered in the corner of the cell unable to take her eyes off the door. As the long night wore on and no one had come near, she had managed to convince herself that Silas and Hetty's threats meant nothing. Now, her stomach churned and she pushed the bowl of gruel aside, although she had eaten nothing since dinner time yesterday.

Despite her fear, she had made up her mind during the long dark night that when she went before the magistrate she would tell everything

– how she had discovered the stolen silver but had been too frightened to tell anyone when Silas had threatened her. She didn't think she'd be able to bring herself to reveal what else he had said – that he knew of her relationship with Jerry and that she had been involved with Mister Oliver. She was sure no one would believe that the master's son had forced himself on her, but would accept Silas's insinuation that she was a willing party to what had gone on. Even if she was found innocent today, revealing that in court would certainly ruin any chance she might have of a future with Jerry. But at least she would be free of this stinking place. They must believe her – they must, she told herself.

But now, with those few words, the old woman had let her know that Silas had friends inside the police station. He would find out if she accused him and he and his aunt would carry out their threats.

Trembling, but defiantly confident that she would find the strength to do the right thing, she was led out of the cell and into the court. She kept her eyes lowered as she was told to stand up in the dock to hear the charge.

After confirming her name and place of residence she squared her shoulders as the magistrate read the charge.

When he asked 'How do you plead?' she lifted her chin and said in a strong, clear voice 'Not guilty.'

There were no further questions and a date was set for her trial a few weeks later. She was told that she would be remanded in custody until then and she was herded downstairs where a warder handcuffed her and looped a chain around her ankles. There were several other prisoners, all similarly restrained. There was only one other female prisoner, a young frightened looking girl. Some of the men looked very menacing, especially one hulk of a man who grinned at Ruby through broken teeth.

They waited in silent misery until the closed carriage drawn by two horses arrived to take them to the jail. The large man had spent the waiting time leering at the two girls and Ruby was pleased to find that the carriage was partitioned off into separate cubicles. She and the other girl were the last to enter, followed by two warders who sat near the door.

The journey seemed to take forever but at last the jolting vehicle stopped and the doors were opened. Ruby jumped down and looked around her, breathing in the comparatively fresh air, but she was not allowed time to take in her surroundings before she and the other girl were addressed by a large woman with a bunch of keys at her waist.

'Come along, you two. No dawdling,' she said in a harsh voice, opening a door to the left of the yard. She led them down a long dimly-lit corridor into a small room with a barred window high up in one wall.

'Wait here,' she said.

As the key turned in the lock, the other girl let out a wail. Despite her own misery and apprehension, Ruby put her arm round her shoulders and tried to comfort her. 'I'm Ruby,' she said. 'What's your name?'

The girl sniffed. 'Emily – but they calls me Emmie.'

'Well, Emmie, at least we're together. Someone told me that, as we're on remand, we'll be put in the association room, not in the cells.' Ruby bit back a sob at the memory of Jerry's words. He had tried to prepare her for what was to come. But his voice had been cold, unemotional. She was sure he thought she was guilty even if he did harbour a little sympathy for her situation. She should have told him the whole story, including the threats Silas and Hetty Catchpole had made. It was too late now but she would have her chance when she came up before the judge. She prayed she would be brave enough to speak out.

She patted Emmie's shoulder and said, 'It will be good to have a friend in here.'

Emmie drew away from her and looked her up and down, taking in the clean dress, the neatly brushed hair. 'I don't know what you're in for but I don't think you'll want to be friends with someone like me – not when you know what I've done.'

'Emmie, I don't care why you're here. It can't be as bad as what they say I've done.'

The wardress returned and looked them both up and down with disdain. 'Here they are, Doctor,' she said.

She removed the chains and handcuffs and the man gave Ruby a cursory examination. When he turned to Emmie, he said, 'This one looks as if she needs feeding up. No hard labour for her.'

'Not for either of them – yet' the wardress said. 'Not while they're on remand anyway.'

'Well, nothing wrong with them – no infections as far as I can see. Better get that one's hair cut though – God knows what's lurking in there.' He gave Emmie a contemptuous smirk and the wardress opened the door for him.

'Right, you two – bath.'

The girls were hustled into a large room containing two baths and told to get undressed. Ruby was happy to comply. She was used to washing all over before dressing each morning and the thought of having a proper bath cheered her up a bit, especially after spending the night in a dank and stinking cell - until she stepped into the freezing water. She didn't need the wardress's harsh command to hurry up.

Emmie, however, refused to get in the water and screamed loudly when the brawny wardress picked her up bodily and dropped her in it.

'Stop that row. You're asking for a beating, you are,' the wardress snapped. But Emmie continued to sob and her sobs grew louder when the woman produced a pair of scissors and began to snip off her tangled curls. Emmie's hair was cut so close to her head that it left bald patches. Running her hand over her head, she cried even louder. She didn't stop until they were dried and dressed and ready to be taken to the dormitory.

Ruby was allowed to dress in her own clothes once more but Emmie's tattered garments were taken away and she was handed a coarse serge dress, striped stockings and a white cap. She looked a different person in her clean clothes and Ruby saw that she was little more than a child, and a very pretty child at that, despite her shorn head. What could she have done to land herself in this dreadful place?

The room they were taken to was low-ceilinged and dimly-lit by two narrow windows which looked out onto a brick wall. Narrow bunks were ranged along one wall and there was a table in the middle of the room. The women who sat round it sewing or knitting barely glanced up at the two new arrivals until the wardress barked at them. Then they slowly put their work down and shuffled to their feet.

'These two are Hinton and Jones. Maggie, show them the ropes.'

She left the room, locking the door behind her. The old woman called Maggie grinned. 'Welcome to paradise, ducks. And what have you two pretty young things been up to?' She let out a cackling laugh and turned to the other women who had taken up their work again. 'Looks like we've got a couple of green'uns here.'

Emmie reached out and clutched Ruby's hand and the woman laughed again.

'No need to be scared, dearie. We're all on remand here – waitin' to go to trial. And, as the law says, we're innocent until proved guilty. Same goes for you two. So, we don't talk about why we're here. We just try to make the best of it 'cause God knows things will get worse.' She pulled two chairs up to the table and gestured them to sit down.

Ruby looked round the room and shivered, grateful that they had allowed her to keep her shawl. Although it wasn't as bad as she had feared, it was grim enough. She wondered how she was going to get through until her trial and then shivered again. Despite assuring herself that the judge would believe her story, she knew that, unless she told them everything, she would be sent to prison for a long time.

Chapter Nineteen

Jeremiah watched from the window as Ruby was taken away. He was sure she knew something. He had seen fear in her eyes and he knew it wasn't because she'd been caught. Someone had threatened her to keep her quiet. And he had a pretty good idea who it was.

He punched the wall in frustration and turned away from the window. He was more determined than ever to bring Silas James and his accomplices to justice. Despite everything, he still loved Ruby and he was convinced she was the victim here. He would do anything to help her - and there was one thing he could do. She probably had no idea how to contact a lawyer and he decided to approach a friend of his. He didn't care if it took all his savings. He also knew that while she was on remand she could receive visitors and he resolved that on his next day off he would go to see her – not as a policeman but as a friend. It was against the rules, but he didn't care. He would make sure that no one at the prison recognised him.

In the meantime he had work to do. Inspector Higgins agreed with Jeremiah that the villains must have had inside help. He just couldn't believe that Ruby was that person.

Doors and windows had been left unlocked and, as the goods stolen were usually small but valuable items which had not been missed for some time, it was hard to put the blame on any one servant. Although Jeremiah knew deep down that Silas was part of the gang, he had put forward the theory that the insider was not a servant but someone who had legitimate access to the houses that had been broken into.

'But you've already arrested an accomplice,' the inspector said.

'Maybe, but she couldn't have been working alone. I believe Ruby Hinton was coerced into helping the gang.'

Inspector Higgins pursed his lips. 'Maybe you're right,' he said. 'Take Constable Knox and canvas the houses that have been targeted. See if any of them have employed painters or other workmen in the recent past.'

Sitting down to compile a list of the most recent burglaries helped to take Jeremiah's mind off Ruby's plight for a little while at least. Then came the long and arduous task of visiting all the houses and interviewing the housekeeper or butler. 'No need to bother the master or mistress of the house,' Inspector Higgins had decreed.

Jeremiah was elated that, at the end of a long, cold day tramping the streets and squares, he and Constable Knox returned to the police station, confident that they'd found their man.

'You're sure about this, Locker?' Inspector Higgins asked when Jeremiah made his report. 'As far as I know this man runs a respectable business. I've employed him in my own house.'

'That may be, sir, but his name cropped up at all the places that have been burgled in the past few months.'

'Better pay him a visit then. But be discreet. And if he is our man, don't give him the chance to warn his confederates.'

* * *

Accompanied by Constable Knox, Jeremiah approached the house at the end of the row of red brick dwellings. The house was larger than those in the rest of the row with a covered yard at the side. As soon as they turned the corner, Jeremiah recognised it. He had been here before when investigating the baby farming scandal.

The woman who lived here was Silas James's mother. She did mind children it was true, but she had seemed respectable enough and Jeremiah had found no evidence of wrongdoing. Nevertheless, he had told the beat constable to keep an eye on the house and report any suspicious activity. And now, here he was calling about another crime. It was too much of a coincidence, he thought. Crime tended to run in families and the man they were looking for could well be related to her. And it was outside this house that he had seen Silas arguing with someone.

Things were beginning to add up, he thought with satisfaction. He knocked on the door, listening to the scuffling and muttered curses from within. He was about to knock again when the door was opened by a scruffy little boy of about seven.

'Wot d'yer want?' he asked, wiping his nose on a ragged sleeve.

'I'd like to speak to Mr Joseph Green if he's home.'

Before the boy could reply a man appeared in the passage behind him. 'What is it this time?' he asked. 'I ain't done nothing. Just 'cause you couldn't pin nothin' on Ma, I s'pose you're after me now.'

'We just want to ask a few questions, that's all,' said Jeremiah. 'If, as you say, you've done nothing wrong, you have nothing to fear.'

'I'm a respectable man, I am. I work hard and make a decent living. No call to go breakin' the law, have I?'

'We'll see about that.'

The man made no move to invite them into the house and Jeremiah began to think he'd get nowhere without actually arresting the man and taking him to the police station. Constable Knox already had the handcuffs ready.

But before he could step forward, a voice from inside the house called out. 'For gawd's sake shut that door, Joe. It's freezing in here.'

Joseph Green made to push the door shut but Jeremiah had his foot over the step. 'We'll talk inside then,' he said.

He followed the man along the narrow passage and into the room at the back, pausing inside the door. The room was hot and stuffy, and he gagged against the mingled smells of stale cooking and imperfectly washed clothes hanging on a line over the range. Several small children sat on the tattered rug in front of the fire while Sarah James nursed a baby in her ample lap.

The woman looked up and grinned. 'Well if it ain't the 'andsome Constable Locker come a-calling.' She noticed the stripes on his arm and gave a loud cackle. 'Sorry, sergeant, I should say. Well, what is it this time?'

'It's nothing, Ma.' Joseph said quickly.

'It's your son I want to talk to.' Jeremiah turned to Joseph. 'I understand you work as a chimney sweep and…'

'So what? I know the law. I don't shove my boys up chimneys no more and if anyone says I do, they're lying.'

Jeremiah was losing patience. The man's bluster made him even more suspicious. And after a few more questions, despite his protestations that he knew nothing, Jeremiah was convinced that Joseph Green was the inside man – and Silas James was implicated too. But who were the actual burglars? Joseph probably knew it was more than his life was worth to peach on his confederates.

Finally, Jeremiah gave up and appeared to let the man think he was satisfied. Without proof he could do nothing and now it was time to hand the case over to the detectives who would no doubt set one of their plain clothes men to watching him.

As they turned the corner on the way back to the police station, Constable Knox spoke for the first time. 'I thought I knew that chap when he came to the door but I was mistaken.'

'You've probably seen him out with his cart around the district,' Jeremiah replied.

'No. The chap I saw was his brother, I'm sure. They're very alike.' He paused. 'You know him too, sergeant. Silas James, one of the footmen employed at Exton House.'

'But Green can't be his brother – different surnames,' Jeremiah said.

'Not unusual – same mother, different fathers I expect.'

Jeremiah could have kicked himself. Why hadn't he picked up on that? And it was in this very street that he'd accosted the footman weeks earlier. When Silas had told him he'd been visiting his mother, he should have made the connection. But his mind had been on the baby farming investigation at the time.

Constable Knox spoke again. 'I didn't like him – sly looking sort of fellow. I'm surprised at Sir Charles taking on someone like that. The housekeeper's his aunt, isn't she? Maybe she spoke up for him and helped him get the job.'

Jeremiah stopped in mid-stride. 'Hetty Catchpole – of course,' he muttered. It was all falling into place now. Ignoring the constable's chatter about the Preston household, he strode on, his mind working furiously. There must be a connection – she had identified the apron as Ruby's to start with, otherwise she would never have been suspected. He had thought it was Silas she was afraid of but his aunt could also be holding something over her. When he'd last seen Ruby in the prison cell he'd been sure she was shielding someone.

Resolved that he would do all he could to prove her innocence, he planned how he could go about it. First, he would have to question the housekeeper again – but carefully so that she didn't realise she was suspected of anything.

* * *

Ruby had thought her little attic room at Exton House was cold but it was nothing to this. At least back there she had adequate bedding. The single blanket they had given her in the prison was almost threadbare and, if it hadn't been for Kitty's shawl, she was sure she would have frozen to death. It was a blessing she'd been allowed to wear her own clothes too.

As well as the cold, the constant noise of doors banging, keys rattling and the cries of the other prisoners woke her constantly and she felt permanently tired.

It was still a relief when the bell sounded to rouse her each morning and, after her meagre breakfast of thin gruel, she was set to work. In some ways she could have been back at Exton House for the work was comfortingly familiar. After cleaning her eating utensils and helping to scrub the floor of the large common room, she was sent to the prison laundry, where at least it was warm.

Although she was allowed visitors, no one came near. Emmie had told her she should ask for a lawyer.

'I don't know any lawyers. Besides, I have no money,' Ruby replied.

'Who's going to speak up for you at your trial then?'

'There's no one. I shall have to speak for myself.' Ruby still hadn't told anyone what she was in prison for and so far the other women had abided by Maggie's rule that they did not question each other about their crimes. Not that they would be too shocked, she supposed. Stealing was a way of life to many poor people – it was the unlucky ones who got caught.

Emmie's words set Ruby thinking. She was allowed to write letters. Perhaps she'd write to Fanny and ask if anyone from Exton House would give her a character reference. It probably wouldn't help but it was worth a try.

She managed to persuade one of the women to let her have pencil and paper in return for doing her share of the cleaning. That evening, thankful that at the Foundling Hospital she had been made to learn her letters, she sat down on her bunk and tried to think what to write. She wanted to tell Fanny the whole story but who knew who might read the letter? Besides, with only one sheet of paper there wasn't room to spill it all out. In the end she wrote a simple and heartfelt message.

"Dearest Fanny, I know you will believe that I am innocent of the wickedness I am accused of. If you, or any of my former friends at Exton House, can find it in your hearts to speak up for me I will be forever grateful."

She ended by asking her friend to thank Kitty for the shawl, signed and sealed it and gave it to the wardress when she came to order "lights out". She knew it would be read by the prison authorities as would any reply she might receive, but there was nothing in it that they could object to.

The next day, as she was wringing out her washcloth after scrubbing the floor, the wardress appeared in the doorway. 'Hinton, visitor for you,' she snapped.

Ruby stood up, a smile lighting her face. It must be Fanny. It was good to know that she had at least one friend left. But as she followed the wardress down the dark corridor to the visitors' room, she realised that it couldn't be her friend. Even if Fanny had received the letter, she wouldn't have been allowed time off from work to visit her.

The wardress opened a door and beckoned Ruby into a small room which was partitioned off with a barred opening giving on to a small space where another wardress sat. Across from her was another barred window framing the figure of a man with his cap pulled down over his forehead.

Ruby gasped and stepped back, her knees shaking. She couldn't see his face but she was sure it was Silas. What was he doing here? Had he come to threaten her again? She took a breath and stepped up to the grille, relaxing as the man moved into the light. He pushed the hat back, revealing his thatch of thick fair hair, and his smile lit up his blue eyes.

She bit back a sob, and leaned against the wall, weak with relief. For a brief moment she really had thought it was Silas. 'Jerry,' she whispered.

He shook his head and put his finger to his lips and she realised why he was wearing a shabby old coat instead of his police uniform. It wasn't much of a disguise and Ruby could hardly believe that he'd braved the displeasure of his superiors to visit her in jail. He shouldn't be here, she thought. She knew he'd be in real trouble if he were found out.

He stepped close to the grille and smiled. 'I thought you'd like to see a friendly face.'

His kindness brought tears to her eyes and she couldn't speak.

'Don't cry, Ruby. Everything is going to be all right. You see, I know you're innocent. The girl I've come to know and love would never be involved in such crimes.'

'Thank you for believing in me, Jerry,' she whispered.

'I've been doing some more investigating and I've found out something which might help you.'

Hope rose in Ruby's heart for a brief moment only to be swamped by fear and despair once more. If he had discovered the truth it

222

could only harm the little Williams boys. Silas James would think Ruby had told all and he would not hesitate to carry out his threat

She began to sob. 'Please, Jerry, let it be. You can't help me – no one can.' Her sobs grew louder and Jeremiah put his hand between the bars, trying to reach out to her. But the space between the two cubicles was too great.

The wardress stood up and turned to Ruby. 'Pull yourself together, girl. No use crying now. Be thankful your young man hasn't abandoned you altogether.'

Ruby's sobs grew louder and the wardress said to Jeremiah, 'Best leave her now.'

He nodded. 'Goodbye, Ruby. I'll come again if I can.'

She said a tearful goodbye and allowed herself to be led away. Her fellow prisoners looked up curiously as she came in, still sobbing. But none of them offered any comfort and she threw herself down on her bunk.

After a while the sobs ceased and she wished she'd been able to talk longer. She wondered what Jerry had found out and how it could possibly help her. It was a comfort to know that he was standing by her. Perhaps she should have confided in him after all. But what could he do? If he returned to Exton House to question Silas and Hetty Catchpole, they would know that she had talked. And then Silas would carry out his threat.

Chapter Twenty

After leaving the prison, Jeremiah went back to the station house and changed back into his uniform. Now that he knew of the connection between Silas James and his chimney sweep half-brother, he had worked out how the gang operated. Joseph Green scoped out the houses he was working in and informed his accomplices of the best time to strike. Hetty Catchpole or Silas left the window open so that the stuff could be hidden until the heat died down.

Jeremiah suspected that they had become nervous of being discovered and had tried to implicate Ruby by using her apron to wrap the silver in. He gave a small laugh of contempt. As if the intelligent girl he had fallen in love with would do something so stupid? His only problem now was deciding whether Ruby knew what had been going on and, if so, why she hadn't told him about it before now.

Jeremiah decided to put his theory to Inspector Higgins, although his boss would probably insist that it should left to the detective branch to look into. He was right of course but, in addition to his genuine desire to help the girl he loved, Jeremiah felt that a successful outcome to the case could only help him in his ambitions to join the detectives himself. Back at the police station, he took a deep breath and knocked on his superior's door.

'I'd like a word about the Hinton case, sir,' he said before he could change his mind.

The Inspector looked up from the papers he was studying. 'Nothing more to do till she comes up for trial, is there?' Higgins said.

'I can't stop thinking about that poor girl,' Jeremiah said. 'I'm sure she was coerced into working with the gang.'

'I sympathise – but you can't allow yourself to get personally involved.'

Jeremiah could hardly confess that he was already involved. They'd probably move him to another division or even throw him off the force altogether. He thought quickly. 'I'm sure she's not in this alone.'

The inspector gave a short bark of laughter. 'Obviously not, Locker. But now we've got her in custody it won't be long before we get it out of her. The rest of the gang will soon be in our hands.'

Jeremiah wasn't so sure. Ruby had been steadfast in not revealing what she knew. But he decided to put the case to his superior. He could authorise a watch on the brothers and, once they were caught in the act and under lock and key, Ruby would have nothing to fear.

He told the inspector of his conviction that Joseph Green, the chimney sweep, had been the inside man. 'His half-brother, Silas, is employed by the Prestons. It's all too much of a coincidence if you ask me.'

Inspector Higgins agreed that it had seemed strange that Exton House was the only one in the square not to have been burgled recently, although the sweep had paid a visit just before the return of the family from Scotland a few months back. 'He must have known the servants would be questioned and obviously didn't want to draw attention to his brother,' he said. After a moment's thought, he continued, 'I must admit, though, your story sounds plausible. Proving it will be difficult.'

Jeremiah stood up eagerly. 'Let me go back to Exton House and question Catchpole, sir. She's the one who accused Ruby Hinton – probably to throw suspicion off her nephew.'

'All right. But if nothing comes of it, you must let it go, Locker. After all, this maid could still be implicated as well.' He waved a hand in dismissal and returned his attention to the papers on his desk. As Jeremiah opened the door, he glanced up and said with the trace of a smile, 'You mustn't let yourself be swayed by a pretty face, you know.'

'No, sir, of course not, sir.' Jeremiah hastily descended the stairs and hailed a cab to Warwick Square. He should have walked but he couldn't bear to delay.

Thank goodness the inspector didn't realise the full extent of his involvement. Besides, he wasn't only being influenced by his feelings for Ruby. He would feel the same about anyone wrongly accused. He knew in his heart she was innocent. It was easy to see now why she was so frightened. Hetty Catchpole was connected to a family of criminals – and she was in a position of authority over the other servants.

* * *

As the day of her trial drew nearer, Ruby grew more apprehensive. A lawyer had been to see her, sent by a friend, he said. When she protested that she couldn't pay him, he told her not to worry. It was all taken care of.

'I don't have any friends,' she said, 'leastways not any with money.'

He just smiled and asked her to go over her story once more.

She wanted to tell the truth, but visions of Silas's cruel smile and his threats against Fanny's little brothers had haunted her dreams. She truly didn't care what happened to her but she couldn't bear the thought of those bright little boys being harmed and the grief it would bring to the Williams family.

So she admitted that the apron was hers and that she knew about the stolen silver hidden in the store room. But she insisted she hadn't put it there and didn't know who was responsible. She could tell he didn't believe her but he nodded and promised to help all he could. 'You have a good record with your employers. Lady Anne tells me she has never found fault with your work. Having a good character might help to mitigate your sentence.' Before he left he expressed his belief that she had somehow been coerced into breaking the law. 'If you decide to

227

confide in me I will make sure you are protected from these villains,' he promised.

But she only shook her head, bursting into tears after he had gone. He couldn't help her, no one could, and she knew that life as a convicted prisoner would be far different from being on remand. Here, she could wear her own clothes, chat with the other women and receive visits. In many ways, it wasn't so different from her life at Exton House. She had rules to obey, discipline was strict, and she had to work hard. She missed Fanny but little Emmie made up for it in a way. Although she still cried herself to sleep each night, during the day Emmie's company helped her to push her dire predicament to the back of her mind. Sometimes they even found something to laugh about.

That all changed a few days after the lawyer's visit. The door of the association room banged open and a new inmate was ushered in. Ruby was sitting at the table sewing. Even on remand, no one was allowed to be idle. She looked up briefly but then went back to her work, only to be jerked upright by the harsh voice.

The new woman stood in front of her, hands on hips. 'Well, well, if it isn't Ruby Hinton.' She turned to survey the room and gave a cackling laugh. 'Did you know our Ruby's a gangster's moll – not the shy little housemaid she's led you to think her.'

Ruby had never seen the woman before and she gasped a protest. But before she could say anything in her defence one of the older women spoke up. 'Leave the girl alone, Maudie. You know we don't talk about why we're here. Come to that, what are you doing back here so soon, eh?'

'Never you mind,' said Maudie, laying a hand on Ruby's arm. She smiled down at her in pretended concern and said, 'Don't worry, I can keep mum – if you can.' The malicious glare in the woman's eyes belied her smile and Ruby realised she had been given a clear warning.

She summoned up her courage. 'It's nobody else's business. Besides, I haven't been found guilty yet.'

'But you will be. My feller Silas tells me that's all they can talk about up at that posh house where you used to work.'

Ruby turned away and picked up her sewing once more. Her heart was beating faster and she was near to tears. But she sniffed them away and tried to appear unconcerned

Over the next few days Maudie constantly taunted Ruby and she began to long for her trial just so that she could get away from the harsh voice of her tormentor.

Her only respite was when they were allocated different duties. To her relief that day, she was sent to work in the laundry with Emmie, while Maudie was on kitchen duty.

'She's really got in for you,' Emmie said. 'Did you know her before?'

'No but she says she's walking out with someone from the house where I worked.

229

Perhaps she thinks she's got cause to be jealous. I can't think of anything else.' Ruby had had time to think up a story to account for the woman's antipathy.

'Well, you won't have to put up with her much longer. She only got seven days for disorderly conduct.'

Ruby realised the woman had probably engineered her arrest knowing she'd be sent to the same prison. At every opportunity she reinforced Silas's threat to the Williams children. Ruby repeatedly tried to convince her that she had said nothing. She could not risk him carrying out his threat. At last Maudie seemed satisfied. 'I get out tomorrow,' she said. 'Silas will be pleased to hear my news.'

But even after Maudie had been released, Ruby couldn't relax. Every time she heard the tramping of feet in the corridor outside followed by the clanking of keys she looked up fearfully. But they didn't come for her and there were no visitors for her either. She began to think she would never see Jerry again and even the lawyer stayed away.

Jerry had hinted that he knew something to help her but she hoped he hadn't uncovered the truth. They would assume she had talked and Silas would have no hesitation in carrying out his threat. If only Jerry would visit. It was hard not knowing what was going on in the outside world.

It was almost a relief when the door was thrown open and her name was called. As well as the chief wardress, two others stood there and, when they fastened the chains around her ankles and wrists again, Ruby knew that she wasn't being taken to the visitors' room this time.

She straightened her shoulders and, with head high, she walked out. The chief wardress led the way and the other two flanked her as she was escorted down long corridors each separated by a locked door. Finally she stood outside in the fresh air but there was no time to savour the illusion of freedom before she was hustled into the closed carriage for the journey to the courthouse.

Inside, her lawyer gave her a smile of encouragement and she looked around for Jerry. Surely he would be there to support her too? But when she spotted him standing to attention near the door, he turned away without a sign of recognition and her heart sank. Although she had repeatedly told herself it would be better if he didn't investigate further, she had clung on to the faint hope that he might be able to discover the truth without causing harm to her friends.

When he hadn't visited her again, she could only think that he had taken her at her word. But when he didn't even glance at her, much less give her an encouraging smile, she began to think he had abandoned her after all.

The door opened and the judge entered. He banged his gavel on the high desk and the usher called for silence. Ruby's trial had begun.

Chapter Twenty One

Jeremiah dared not look at Ruby. He did not want to offer her false hope and, after that one visit, he had kept away from the prison while he pursued his investigations. He hoped she didn't think he had abandoned her. Now, he could only rely on his lawyer friend to do his part when it came to the defence.

In his quest to prove Ruby innocent he had been relentless in his search for the truth, questioning the servants at Exton House more rigorously than before. Sir Charles had not been at all happy about it. 'Just a few minor points to clear up,' Jeremiah said. 'The trial is almost upon us and we need to make sure we have all the facts.'

Sir Charles had reluctantly agreed after stipulating that there must be as little disruption to the household as possible.

Jeremiah, not wishing to arouse Hetty Catchpole's suspicions, started by talking to the kitchen maids. They both insisted that Ruby had no opportunity to help the burglars. 'She was as scared as we were,' Annie said, telling him about the heavy chest they had pushed against their bedroom door each night after the watchman had been assaulted.

Kitty, who was sitting at the table chopping vegetables, gave a little exclamation. 'I've just remembered something. I'm sure it was the night the house next door was burgled. Ruby wasn't well and I went down to get her a drink.'

'Did you see or hear anything?'

Kitty hesitated. 'I saw someone.'

'Why didn't you mention this before,' Jeremiah asked.

'I didn't think anything of it till now. We were all upset the next morning because the police were here.'

'Who was it?'

'I don't like to say.' The maid gave a frightened look at Mrs Andrews. But Jeremiah motioned her to continue.

'Well, I made some tea for Ruby and was just going upstairs when I heard the back door close so I hid in the broom cupboard. I knew I shouldn't be downstairs at that time of night. I thought it was Mr Phelps doing his rounds, making sure everything was locked up and I didn't want him to see me.'

'And was it Mr Phelps?' Jeremiah could hardly contain his impatience.

'No, it was Silas. I remember wondering where he'd been.' She glanced at Mrs Andrews again and gave a nervous giggle. 'I thought he'd been out to meet a woman. But he said later he'd been to see his ma.'

Jeremiah nodded and asked Kitty to continue. 'Nothing else to tell. After he'd turned out the gas and gone upstairs, I went up and gave Ruby her tea.'

* * *

Hetty had been enjoying a rare day off and was on her way back to Exton House after visiting her sister. She was in a good mood, savouring the thought of the coins in her pocket after another successful job.

Her position at Exton House gave her access to all the gossip in the square both upstairs and downstairs. And she had just "helped" another unfortunate maid out of her predicament by persuading her sister Sarah to accept a further addition to her overcrowded household. In return the girl had handed over a whole year's wages to ensure that her child was well looked after. Hetty's share of the money would be added to her growing retirement nest egg.

She tightened her lips and her mood darkened. She would be on her way to that cottage by the sea now if that stupid girl hadn't poked her nose in, although she was sure Ruby hadn't told anyone what she had discovered. Hetty was still wondering how the police had latched on to the goings on at Exton House and she ground her teeth in frustration. That stupid Silas had probably been bragging while in his cups. It was only her quick thinking that had shifted suspicion to Ruby. She grinned in satisfaction. Sarah had assured her that Silas's friend Maudie had put the fear of God into the girl.

'She won't peach, you can count on it,' Sarah said. 'We'll just have to lie low for a bit.

Joe's keeping his nose clean too for the time being. He's been on pins since that copper came round.'

'Let's hope he don't connect your Joe with me. You know what a suspicious lot they are,' Hetty said.

'No, you're all right. That girl's locked up and she won't be getting out any time soon and besides, who'd believe the little slut.'

Hetty was reassured and, as she crossed the stable yard and entered through the back door, she straightened her hat and assumed her usual demeanour of the reliable and devoted servant. She swallowed the mint she'd been sucking and congratulated herself that none of her fellow servants would guess she had spent the afternoon drinking gin and exchanging gossip with her sister.

She hung up her coat and hat and donned her apron and was about to go up the back stairs when Kitty came out of the kitchen. 'Oh, Mrs Catchpole, that policeman's here again.'

Hetty's heart began to thump. 'What does he want?'

'Same old questions. Waste of time if you ask me,' the girl said.

'Where is he now?'

'He's with Mr Phelps. Wants to speak to you now. I told him it was your day off but he said he'd wait.'

Hetty smoothed her apron. 'All right, Kitty. Nothing to worry about. I expect they want me to give evidence at the trial.' But as she opened the door to the butler's room she couldn't help a little flicker of alarm.

* * *

Now, Jeremiah replayed his questioning of the housekeeper in his mind as he listened to the prosecution barrister outlining his case against Ruby. He stole a glance at her and swallowed the lump in his throat. She looked so small and defenceless up there. How he wished he could comfort her, reassure her that everything would be all right. But, despite knowing that Hetty Catchpole would soon be called as a witness, he knew that things could still go badly for the girl he loved.

Now it was his turn to take the stand and he took a deep breath before mounting the steps and taking the oath.

Jeremiah had sworn to tell the truth. But, although he had to explain that it was the discovery of the maid's apron that had led to Ruby's arrest, he didn't mention the scarlet ribbon he'd found. It wasn't relevant to the case so why complicate matters? At least that's what he told himself. He wanted to mention the noise he'd heard as he passed the Exton House stable yard soon after the burglary, although he wasn't sure how that would help Ruby. Perhaps the less said the better.

* * *

Ruby listened to all those people talking about her and what she was supposed to have done but she couldn't take it in. It was as if they were talking about someone else. From her place in the dock she gazed down at the blur of faces and felt a little dizzy. If only they'd let her sit down. She grabbed the railing in front of her and forced herself to pay attention. That lawyer, whose name she could not remember, had stood up now, a sheaf of papers in his hand.

He cleared his throat and began to speak. 'The prosecution has told you that the prisoner in the dock is part of a gang of ruthless thieves who have ransacked many houses in the area. She has aided and abetted them by concealing the stolen goods on the premises where she worked.'

He paused and then went on, 'I put it to you that the opposite is true. Here is an innocent young woman, a hard-working servant in a respectable household. She insists on her innocence and, while we cannot just take her word, you must take into account that the only evidence we have is the fact that the some of the 'booty' was wrapped in an apron belonging to the accused. I put it to you that anyone in that household could have taken Ruby Hinton's apron from the laundry basket and used it to discredit her.' His eyes swept over the jury and the packed courtroom.

After another pause, he answered his own question. 'She did not do what the prosecution has alleged. And I will prove it to you.' He turned to the usher. 'Call Hetty Catchpole.'

The cry echoed round the courtroom and there was a rustle of interest as the housekeeper came in and mounted the witness stand. She took the oath, speaking in a quiet voice, her eyes lowered deferentially.

As the lawyer started questioning her, despair overtook Ruby and the voices faded away. Locked in misery she started when Hetty's voice rang through the courtroom. 'Yes, I identified the girl's apron. And I also told the policeman that I had seen Hinton coming out of the storeroom on more than one occasion.'

'Did she have a reasonable explanation for her presence?'

'Well, one time she said she was fetching something for Mrs Andrews but it was past midnight and everyone else was in bed.' Hetty looked round the court defiantly. 'What else would she be doing down in the basement where she had no reason to be?'

'Just answer the question, Mrs Catchpole. You must not make statements like that,' the lawyer admonished.

'I'm sorry, your honour. I only speak as I find.'

Ruby leaned forward, crying out. 'She's trying to make me look bad. Mrs Andrews did send me down – ask her.'

The judge interrupted. 'You must not speak unless asked to do so. Your turn will come.' He nodded to the barrister to continue.

Ruby leaned back, relieved. Surely Mrs Andrews would speak up for her. But when she came to the stand she said she couldn't remember what night it was. 'I'm always sending the maids on errands – how can I be expected to recall who and when?' she protested.

The barrister did not pursue the matter and Ruby was disappointed when he dismissed Mrs Andrews without further questions. Instead, to her surprise, he called the next witness, Police Sergeant Jeremiah Locker.

* * *

Jeremiah watched Hetty Catchpole leave the courtroom and gave a small smile of satisfaction. He had already instructed Constable Knox to keep an eye on her and he was confident that she would soon be under arrest, along with her two nephews and other members of the gang.

It had taken a long time to gather all the evidence and make the arrests but he was confident now that Ruby would soon be released. As he took the stand, he glanced up at Ruby with an encouraging smile, pleased to see that the colour had come back to her cheeks.

After going through the usual procedure the barrister said, 'It is somewhat unusual for a member of the police force to be called as a defence witness, isn't it?'

'Yes, sir.'

'Will you tell us in your own words exactly how you came to be in this position then.'

Jeremiah nodded and explained how he had become involved in the investigation. Of course, he couldn't reveal that it was love for Ruby which had made him so determined to prove her innocence. But now that he had the proof he needed, he confidently explained how the small pieces of evidence had come together.

'I was aware that there had been a spate of burglaries in the area so I was especially vigilant as I made my rounds. As I passed Exton House I noticed that the gates to the stable yard were open. Although it was late, there was a light in the coachman's quarters above the stables. I thought that he was waiting up until the son of the house returned. I knew from previous conversations with Williams, the coachman that Oliver Preston sometimes stayed out late. All the same I had a good look round to make sure nothing was amiss. All was quiet so I decided to resume my beat. But, as I started to walk away I heard a noise. I waited for a while but when it was not repeated I concluded it had been a cat and I continued on my way.'

Jeremiah continued his story – how he had noted Silas James's frequent absences from the house and how, after his talk with Williams about the window being left open, he had become suspicious. 'Exton House had not been broken into - the only one in the square to escape. At first I thought the open window might have been an oversight on the part of the butler who is responsible for locking up. But Williams told me that Mr Phelps is very conscientious and always double-checked. He became suspicious too and together we kept watch for several nights. What we saw led us to apply for a search warrant at Exton House.'

'Why were you so convinced that Miss Hinton wasn't involved?'

'At first it was just a feeling that something didn't add up. The prisoner' Jeremiah glanced up at Ruby and continued, '– the prisoner was vehement in her protestations of innocence. But she knew something and I wondered if she had been coerced into silence.' He told of the bruises he had seen on Ruby's wrists and her nervousness when being questioned. 'I was sure she was hiding something – and not her involvement with the gang. It was fear keeping her silent.'

As he spoke, Ruby began to feel a small spark of hope. When she was called to give evidence she made up her mind that now she must tell everything she knew. The lawyer had impressed on her that her only hope lay in telling the whole story. But until now she had been intimidated by Silas and Hetty's threats against the little Williams boys.

Jeremiah's speaking up for her had made her brave.

Hesitantly she told of finding the stolen silver. 'I would have spoken up then,' she said, clasping her hands on the rail in front of her and leaning forward. 'I knew Silas meant what he said. I wasn't scared for myself, sir, but I couldn't let anything happen to Fanny and her little brothers.' She began to sob. 'I wanted to do the right thing, really I did.'

The wardress put and hand on her shoulder.. 'Quiet, Hinton,' she whispered, but her voice was sympathetic.

She continued to sob quietly, the voices faded away and she felt the room swaying. The rest of the trial passed in a blur - Kitty's testimony and the barrister's summing up, followed by the jury's "not guilty" verdict.

The courtroom erupted and the judge banged his gavel, crying for order. The wardress took her arm, more sympathetically now, and urged her to sit down.

Chapter Twenty Two

It was all over and Ruby stood looking about her in a daze. Silas and Mrs Catchpole had been arrested along with the rest of the gang. At least she could be surenow that Fanny's little borthrs were safe. But was she really free? She couldn't take it in. Despite Jerry's assurances, she hadn't dared to believe she would be acquitted. What should she do now?

The wardress looked at her kindly. 'Well, dearie, it's not often I get to see an acquittal,' she said. 'You can go home now, put it all behind you.'

But where was home? The Foundling Hospital and Exton House were the only places she had ever called home. And she certainly couldn't go back to Exton House.

She knew no one in London besides her fellow servants – and Jerry. Her heart swelled at the thought of him. He had believed in her, fought for her, risked his career to find out the truth. She loved him and, she thought, he loved her too.

Was there a future for them? She admired his ambition and wished him well in his hoped-for promotion to the detective force. He'd be good at it too, she knew. But he wouldn't get very far married to a suspected criminal. There would always be some people who'd look at her suspiciously, even though she'd been acquitted. No. she must put all thoughts of a future with Jeremiah behind her.

She hurried out of the courthouse, anxious to get away before Jerry could catch up with her. She stopped when she reached the corner of the busy street and stood looking about her. Where could she go? She began to wander aimlessly, jostled by the crowds, unheeding of the curses as she bumped into people intent on their own busy lives.

She must have walked for hours, not sure where she was even, until she turned a corner and found herself outside the park gates – the park where Jerry had declared his love and where she had been so happy for such a brief time. She entered and sat on a bench. It was bitterly cold, spring still far away. But she savoured her freedom, reliving those wonderful moments in Jerry's arms, his passionate kisses and the bittersweet thought that she would never feel such happiness again.

As she shivered in the cold air, glad that she still had Kitty's shawl, a shadow fell across her and she looked up to see Jerry smiling down at her. 'I've been looking for you,' he said, sitting down beside her and taking her hand. 'I have something of yours.' He reached into his pocket and pulled out the red ribbon.

'How did you get it? Mrs Catchpole took it away from me.'

'So she was the one dropped it.'

'What do you mean?'

'Never mind now.' He took her hand and wound the ribbon round her fingers. 'It's a bit crumpled. I'll have to buy you another.'

'I don't want another – I'll treasure this one, crumpled or not.' She looked up at him, her eyes misty. 'How did you know where to find me?'

'I guessed you had nowhere to go and I wanted to help you. But when I looked round you'd gone. Then I remembered that day and I had a feeling you'd come here.'

'I was reliving a happy memory,' she said, smiling, her heart swelling at the thought that he had come to find her. But she still couldn't believe there really was a future for them. He had his career, but she had no job and no home to go to. She covered her face with her hands and gave a little sob. 'Oh, Jerry what am I going to do? I know I'm free now but I've got no home, no family...I can't go back to the house. I'd love to see Fanny again and her little brothers but I can't face them all.'

'You don't have to. I'll look after you.'

She looked up at him. 'I didn't think you'd still want to know me.'

'How could you think that? I knew along you were innocent.'

'But after everything that's happened...?' She couldn't go on.

'Nothing that happened was your fault.' He put his hand over her mouth to silence her as she was about to protest. 'You know I love you, my sweet Ruby.' He raised her hand to his lips and kissed it tenderly.

A little hope burgeoned in her breast. Was he really thinking of a possible future for them? But he didn't know everything. She couldn't acknowledge their love and still hold on to this dreadful secret. It was now time to tell him everything and if he rejected her, then…

She took a deep breath. 'I have to tell you something, Jerry.'

'You don't have to – I trust you,' he replied.

'I'll feel better if you know – even if you never want to see me again.'

He shook his head. 'I love you, Ruby. Nothing you could tell me…'

Now it was her turn to put her hand over his lips. 'Let me speak, please,' she said. And before she could change her mind, she found herself pouring it all out – Oliver's assault, the resulting pregnancy and the horror of the miscarriage.

'Mrs Catchpole knew. I thought she was being kind keeping my secret but now I realise she just wanted something to hold over me.' She began to sob as the story came to a close.

So that explained the blood-stained apron, Jerry thought, taking her in his arms and cradling her head against his chest. 'My poor darling. I had no idea what you'd been through.' His voice shook with anger. 'These rich young men who think they can do what they like and get away with it. First my poor sister, now you.'

246

'I could live with what Oliver had done to me but when I realised Silas knew about it, I was so ashamed. And then he threatened to tell you…' She gave a shuddering sob. 'I told him he could say what he liked. I wasn't afraid of him. But then he started on the Fanny and the boys.'

Jerry lifted her chin and kissed her. 'You were so brave to speak up. No one will ever hurt you again – I promise,' he said.

Her sobs subsided and she returned his kiss. How could she have doubted him? But she shook her head. 'What about your career, Jerry? That inspector won't like you being involved with someone like me.'

'Don't worry about him. Yes, it's true I'm ambitious but I'd give it all up just to be with you, Ruby, my love.'

'My love, he'd called her 'my love.' She smiled up at him. 'Jerry, you don't know how happy it makes me to hear you say that. But I know how much your police career means to you…'

'Not as much as you mean to me,' he said, holding her closer. This time the kiss left her in no doubt that he meant what he said. It was everything she'd dreamed of as she lay in her cold lonely prison cell. It was deep and warm, arousing feelings in her that she had thought she'd never experience again.

He pulled away and smiled down at her. 'Does that convince you?'

She nodded and leaned towards him. Cold as it was, she felt she could sit here forever, wrapped in his arms, feeling his heart beating against hers. But she couldn't. She still had nowhere to stay tonight.

'What are we going to do?' she asked, holding her breath for his reply. Did he expect her to go back to Exton House? The lawyer had told her that Sir Charles and Lady Anne had kept her job open for her. But she couldn't bear the thought of being the subject of endless gossip whether below or above stairs.

'It's all arranged, my love. My colleague Sergeant Harris has a room in his house. His wife is happy to put you up.'

'That's kind. But I'll have to find another job.' She gasped. 'Who will employ me once they know about the court case?'

Jeremiah hugged her to him. 'You mustn't worry about that. You won't need a job when we're married.' He paused and an uncertain look crossed his face. 'You will marry me, won't you?'

Ruby looked up into his face, her own eyes reflecting the love she saw there. 'Of course I will – if you're sure.'

'I've never been more sure of anything,' he said, kissing her again.

Ruby melted into his arms and returned the kiss before pushing him away. 'No, Jerry, you can't – marry me, I mean.'

'What do you mean?'

'The scandal, Jerry. Oh, I know you said you don't care about that, but think of your job – you want to join the detectives, don't you? They won't have you if you've been involved with a suspected criminal.'

'No one will know – not where we're going,' Jerry said. 'Ruby, listen to me. I love you and I want to marry you. Nothing and nobody will stand in the way of that.'

Her heart swelled at his words and she wanted so much to believe him. But if she agreed, would he one day come to resent her for thwarting his ambitions? She couldn't bear the thought.

She should refuse him, go back to Exton House and brave the curious stares of her fellow servants, even put up with Mister Oliver's attentions. It wouldn't be so bad. The scandal would soon blow over and Mister Oliver would marry his Amelia and go to live in Yorkshire.

'Well, what do you say?' Jerry was gripping her shoulders and gazing into her eyes.

She knew she should say no, but seeing the look in his eyes, she just couldn't. She leaned against him, her cheek against his and said quietly, 'Yes, Jerry, I will marry you.'

She gave herself up to his kiss, thinking herself the happiest and luckiest girl in the world. Suddenly, something he had said came back to her and she leaned away from him. 'What did you mean – where we're going?'

He grinned at her. 'Didn't I tell you? Inspector Higgins has approved a transfer to another police force. I'm going home, Ruby, and you're coming with me.'

'Home?'

'Back to Norfolk, Ruby. I've been transferred to Norwich police station. And you can stay with my parents until we get married.'

'But what about your family? Are you sure they'll welcome me?'

'They'll love you as I do,' he assured her. He went on to tell her about his sister and how she had died. 'My family are poor, Ruby,' he said, 'but what they lack in material things they more than make up for in other blessings – love and kindness.' He kissed her again and she snuggled up to him, listening entranced as he spoke of the village where he had grown up. He had told her before of the cluster of cottages round the village green and pond, the wide East Anglian skies and she tried to imagine living there, away from the noise and grime of the big city.

He finished speaking and when she was silent he tilted her chin up so that her eyes met his. 'What's wrong, my love? Oh please, say you'll come with me.'

'Of course I will, didn't I tell you I wanted to move to the country.' She smiled but her eyes clouded and she said, 'Are you really sure though. I still can't believe…'

He put his arms around her and pulled her to him once more. 'I'm sure. I fell in love with you the moment I first saw you and you have never been out of my thoughts since then. The thing is, are you sure, my love? I know it's a big step for you to leave all that's familiar and go among strangers.'

'There's nothing here for me, Jerry. Besides, I don't care where I am so long as I'm with you.'

She stood up and took his hand and together they left the park and set out on their new life together.

The End

About the Author

After 22 years of handling other people's books while working as a library assistant, Roberta Grieve decided it was time to fulfil a long-held ambition and starting writing her own. On taking early retirement she began writing short stories and magazine articles with some success. She then turned to novels and her first, 'Abigail's Secret', was published in 2008. Since then she has had seven more historical romances published as well as eight short novels published as large print paperbacks.

Roberta lives in a small village near Chichester, Sussex, and when not writing enjoys walking her son's dog.

bookswelove.com